I0720324

SWEETHEART FOR THE SEAL

ALEXIS ABBOTT

PATHFORGERS PUBLISHING

© 2018 Pathforgers Publishing.

All Rights Reserved. This is a work of fiction. Names, characters, places and incidents are the product of the author's imaginations. Any resemblances to actual persons, living or dead, are entirely coincidental.

This book is intended for sale to Adult Audiences only. All sexually active characters in this work are over 18. All sexual activity is between non-blood related, consenting adults. This is a work of fiction, and as such, does not encourage illegal or immoral activities that happen within.

Cover Design by Wicked Good Covers. All cover art makes use of stock photography and all persons depicted are models.

More information is available at Pathforgers Publishing.

Content warnings: kidnapping, attempted sexual assault (not by hero), natural disaster

Wordcount: 54,000 Words

Get an EXCLUSIVE book, **FREE** just as a thank you for signing up for my newsletter! Plus you'll never miss a new release, cover reveal, or promotion!

http://alexisabbott.com/newsletter

I feel the guard's thrashing slow down as my sleeper hold chokes the consciousness from him, and soon, he goes limp in my arms. As he does, I kneel down and lay him flat on the pristine, tiled floor of the balcony overlooking the lush Colombian jungle.

I check the guard's unconscious body and take the keys off him. If all is going according to plan, I have about thirty seconds to hide the body somewhere that won't get checked for another couple hours. According to our floor plan of this drug lord's estate, that would be the laundry room just inside the doors to my right, second room on the left.

Off in the distance, I hear the sounds of shouting and gunfire. Right on time. The rest of my team is staging an assault of the estate from the south side, along the road between two densely jungled mountains that pour a steady stream of mist onto the drug lord's massive estate grounds.

They're going to draw the bulk of the fire, and I'm going to make my way through the manor and deal with the target.

I've been out in this jungle for weeks, long before the rest of my squad showed up. It's all part of the plan— I have to be a specter, a shadow that can't be so much as suspected out here while the rest of the operation goes according to plan. I memorized the lay of the land so closely that it might as well be my hometown back in the Appalachians. I know its rhythm. I even know some of the drug lord's patrolmen by their first names. None of them so much as dream that I've been lurking in the woods this whole time, scoping them all out and learning their schedules. They didn't suspect as much when I smuggled myself into the compound in a bag of rice, and they don't suspect as much now that my squadmates are raining fire down on them at the front gates.

I'm a Navy SEAL. Perfection is my job.

After checking it, I slip into the manor through the doorway. Like clockwork, the hallway is empty, as expected. I carry the body to the laundry room and slip it behind one of the machines, where he'll be out cold for a long while yet. Long enough for me to do what I need and get out of here.

But from here on out, things will get messy. I can

get all the way into a drug lord's compound without raising the alarm with no problem, given enough planning. Getting into his bedroom during a full-scale assault is another beast.

I only have a short time in private, and I take advantage of it. I take the weapons out of the bag strapped to my back and assemble them — two pistols and my submachine gun — guns that I know so intimately that I could assemble them in my sleep. I don't have the benefit of an assault rifle like my squad does.

Fortunately, I won't need it.

The same training was drilled into each and every one of us. Nothing short of perfection is expected, and we aim to deliver. It's all to protect the ones we love back home.

I don't have much of a family back home. Dad's gone, and Mom keeps to herself these days. That would be more than enough to keep me going, but there's one other face that hasn't left the back of my mind since the day I shipped off. As I finish loading my weapons, the thought of seeing her again crosses my mind for what must be the millionth time. It's what keeps me comforted at night, keeps me pushing myself to my limits and beyond every time I train.

The funny part is: I don't even know if she remembers me.

That doesn't matter right now.

I have to stay focused.

I get low and make my way to the door again, putting my ear to it. I hear heavy footsteps outside, as expected. I wait for them to pass just a couple steps by, then slide out of the doorway. Quiet as a shadow, I see the guard's back, and my body moves with machine-like precision. I wrap my arms around his neck and give him the same treatment as the other guy stashed behind the washing machines, then put him in the same hiding spot.

I'm on borrowed time now.

Because the second the other guards out there realize the patrolman isn't coming back out of the hallway, there's a chance they'll catch on to what's happening.

Sure, it will be too late for them by then. But it would be a lot messier.

Submachine gun on my back, suppressor on my pistol, I leave the safety of the hallway and use a hand mirror to check around the corner of the hall into the staircase it leads to. My pistol is out, and I'm poised to fire as quickly as I need to.

I'm taking what are essentially servant's passages up the manor. The rich crime lords this place entertains don't want to see the staff any more than is necessary, so there are discreet passages built into the infrastructure to let them move around without being seen much. That makes these halls a huge security risk, and most players who have survived the game long enough to understand that lesson have the routes well guarded.

Even so, there's no cleaner way up to my destination, so it's a chance I have to take.

Around the corner of the first staircase I get up, I hear footsteps coming my way, and I ready my aim. An old man rounds the corner carrying a basket of laundry, and his face goes white at the sight of me. I step forward, putting a finger to my lips as he stands aside for me. I don't kill civilians, period.

But I can't just let him go free, either — I can't take any chances. I gesture for him to drop his laundry, then I turn him around and bind his wrists behind his back before proceeding upstairs.

This time, I hear heavier boots heading my way. I drop to one knee and ready myself.

A moment later, two guards round the corner on the stairwell I'm heading toward, and I fire two bullets. The men hit the ground without so much as a word, guns falling from their grip, and I hear someone shouting behind them in Spanish. The time for caution and the element of surprise is gone.

I take out my submachine gun and race forward, diving just in time for the third man to pop around the corner. I tackle him to the ground and twist his gun out of his arms while I take aim at the fourth man standing above us, who's midway through raising his gun. With a quick burst of bullets, I drop him, then use my elbow to knock out the man I'm grappling with. My heart rate has barely increased by the time I stand back up and proceed.

Someone has probably heard the fighting by now. I have even less time to work with. I have complete faith that my team will pull through for me. If they don't, I'm already dead. But I don't need to worry about that. If I didn't have total confidence in them, I wouldn't have agreed to do this.

That's just part of being a SEAL.

On the last flight below the floor where my target's office is located, I stop climbing the stairs and move out to the hallway. There are three more guards moving away from me, but as soon as I step into the hallway, they turn and see me. They don't have time to react before a few quick, precise bursts of fire from my gun put them down.

I breeze by them to the nearest window, the one I studied in excruciating detail from afar. I climb out so smoothly that it looks like I've been practicing for months, and I start climbing the stonework up to the next floor. My target probably has guards in front of his door by now, as well as around him — it's my job to find the weak point.

I make my way up to the balcony jutting out from the rear exit of his office, and I can hear men speaking in Spanish, asking each other if they have word on the identity of their attackers. Maybe the element of surprise isn't totally gone, yet. If my target knew the SEALs were after him, he might already be trying to make his escape.

My target is an odd one. He's not even Colombian — his name is Steven Bennett, hardly the type you'd expect to be running a drug ring in the heart of Colombia. He's an American former DEA agent who went rogue and used his connections down south to climb to the top of a kingdom of cocaine and blood. His associates call him *El Cocodrilo*.

I climb to the edge of the balcony and watch the guards from below. If one of them looks down, I'm dead. It's a risk I have to take. The moment their idle, anxious strolling makes their backs turn to me, I hoist myself up and over the edge of the stone railing.

The two men turn to me immediately, but I'm already mid-lunge on one of them. I tackle him to the ground and wrestle him into my grasp while the other aims his gun at us, hesitating. I twist around and use the man as a human shield, which distracts him long enough for me to get a shot off at him. The moment he falls, I knock out the man in my arms and head for the door to the drug lord's office.

I take out a stun grenade. I don't want a bloodbath, no matter how vicious the men inside are, and even though I could choose to mow down as many as possible with my guns. That's just not how I operate.

Unless there's another gun pointing at me, I don't fire.

I pull the pin on the grenade and toss it into the door. I hear a number of shouts from inside moments before it goes off with an ear-shattering bang, accompanied by a blinding flash. It's my cue.

I move in, submachine gun out, shouting in Spanish at the crazed, confused group of people inside. The room is lavish, furnished with elegant desks and couches that I haven't seen the likes of in the houses of admirals in my own branch of the military.

"Weapons down! Hands up! Everyone!"

There are three guards by the front door, two flanking me, and *El Cocodrilo* himself not far from where I'm standing. I have options here, once again.

In my experience, the best solution is the simplest.

Steven '*El Cocodrilo*' Bennett is about five paces in front of me, wearing a designer suit that doesn't do much to hide how physically weak of a man he is. I lunge forward, grab him, and I have a gun to his head before the rest of the room can get its bearings.

"Fuck-" Bennett has time to curse before I yank him back, moving toward the door. The guards start to raise their weapons, but I make it clear that one wrong move on their part means Bennett dies. It's a bluff, but one that no bodyguard is willing to take.

"The men attacking your compound are US Navy

SEALs," I shout in Spanish as I move back with my target. "Bennett is ours. You have nothing left to fight for."

"Kill him, you fuckers!" Bennett orders them through gritted teeth. They hesitate, and for one heart-stopping moment, it's a very real possibility that the room is about to get very chaotic and bloody.

Finally, I make it to the door back to the balcony, and nobody stops me. I shut it, and I'm alone with Bennett.

"Cock-suckers," he groans.

"Arms up," I order him as I pat him down, stripping him of a couple of hidden weapons on his person before binding his wrists behind his back. He's a doughy man with gray hair at the temples and not a scrap of remorse in his eyes.

"How do you plan on getting me out of here, boy scout?" he chuckles at me. "You're better off putting a bullet in my head right now."

"I could leave you here and let one of your subordinates do that for you," I reply matter-of-factly. "Somehow, I don't think letting your compound get raided is a good look for a drug lord. You've had your fun, Bennett." I take out the climbing gear I brought with me and show it to him before harnessing him to me. "It's my job to take you to justice, not the reaper. There'll be time for that later."

~

*H*ours later, I'm sitting in the back of a black transport helicopter with the rest of my squad, getting airlifted out of Colombia and back home. Spirits are high — I can't keep a smile off my face at seeing the other three of them after so long, even though all our faces are concealed by our masks. We clap hands together firmly, half-laughing as we talk to each other.

"Was starting to get worried about you up there, Anderson," says Walker. "Didn't want your four-year anniversary to be your last."

"I'll be damned if some pencil-necked turncoat takes me down," I chuckle. "How'd things go at the front door?"

"Cooper took a bullet to the shoulder, but otherwise good," he says.

Cooper gives me a thumbs-up, and I nod.

"And that wraps up the operation," I say, nodding. "Bennett neutralized, his lieutenants dealt with, and his contacts scattered. Well done, everyone."

"Until they sic us on the next handful of crime lords down here," Parker grunts, and Walker nods.

"Maybe I'll take the role of the guy stuck surviving in the jungle for a couple weeks. What do you say, Anderson?"

"On the contrary, you might not have a choice," I say, and they all look at me, perplexed.

"What do you mean?"

"Being in the jungle a couple weeks gives you a lot of time to think things over," I say, leaning forward. "But I won't get all sentimental on you. Short version is, I'm taking some personal time. Hopefully not long, but I've got some business I need to take care of back up north."

"Damn, well alright," Walker says. "No complaints from us — God knows you've earned it, if any of us have."

"Agreed," Cooper and Parker say at the same time.

"What is it, though?" Walker adds. "Family?"

I crack a smile.

"Something like that."

Her face is still in my mind, fresh as the day I left her. Crystal-clear.

CRYSTAL

"Mommy, Mommy!"

I look up from the bagged loaf of bread in my hands, squinting and straining to listen for what sounds like my little daughter's sweet, plaintive voice from across the house. I set down the bread and put a hand on my hip, turning toward the kitchen entryway and focusing in.

It's one of those many, many quirks of motherhood everybody failed to warn me about: that I would become so overly-sensitized to the sound of my child's own voice that sometimes, I just might imagine hearing it in the breeze or mixed in with the songs on the radio.

When you're a mother, you grow very, very accustomed to picking out your own child's face, her voice, even her own particular giggle out of a crowd. Ever since she was a tiny baby whose only communication was to scream and cry, I have been able to so easily distinguish the meaning and intensity of every screech and whimper and coo.

She's nearly four now, so I'm pretty damn good at deciphering what pitch of her voice means she's excited or happy and which tone means she's hurt or upset and needs my attention ASAP.

Her innocent, lisping voice is constantly in my mind, as she tends to take up at least ninety percent of my thoughts at any given time. Not that I'm complaining. My daughter is an angel, the best three-year-old best friend and coworker I could have ever imagined.

That's right: coworker. I know how silly that sounds to most people, but considering the fact that my job is to run a small daycare center out of my home, it makes a tad bit more sense. Yes, Dakota is one of the kids I spend my days watching, teaching, feeding, and snuggling with alongside other people's children, but she's also my little helper a lot of the time.

Which is partly why I'm listening so intently for her voice right now; because it's a quarter 'til nine and that's our usual prescribed breakfast time, and Dakota usually helps me with the food prep.

Not that I even have to ask her to.

She's always been a strangely helpful, thoughtful child. If I'm doing chores around the house, even gross things like scrubbing a toilet or taking out the garbage, she jumps right in to help me however she can

I love spending time with her, especially one-on-one, since occasionally I do worry that it might hurt her feelings having to share her mom's attention with other children at the daycare. But she's always so upbeat, so even-keeled, that from time to time I have to wonder if she might even be more mature than some of my parent friends.

I listen carefully, zoning out all other sounds in the house: the news playing on the television in the den, the children's animated show playing on the television in the playroom, the rain lightly pattering against the windows and the roof, and the omnipresent hum of kitchen appliances. And through the din, I hear it again.

"Mommy!" I hear her cry out, this time clear as a whistle. I stride out of the kitchen with a businesslike briskness, clearing the corridor in a few broad steps to poke my head around the corner into the playroom area. My daughter is perched on the arm of the light pink mid-century modern sofa I found at an estate sale a year ago, and she's got one eyebrow pricked up, her sweet, round little face wearing an expression of pure sass.

With her pudgy arms folded over her chest, she glances up at me and then pointedly rolls her eyes to stare at the two little boys curled up on the woven rug on the floor. The two of them are coloring with crayons, which is perfectly fine, except that they keep snapping the crayons in half in between inspired scribbles. With every *SNAP*, I see Dakota wince a little, and even though it's almost funny enough for me to smile at, I understand her annoyance. The crayons are meant to be shared among all the kids I watch here, but *Kota* has always been possessive and protective over the toys and playthings I've accumulated over the years. She's like my little deputy, keeping her hawk-eyed focus on preventing theft or vandalism or whatever you might call the very serious and unforgivable crime of breaking crayons in half.

"Mommy, I've been *calling* you," my daughter sighs, poking out her plump little bottom lip in a pout. She looks up at me with this big, round green eyes that remind me of the color of the choppy waves of the Atlantic under stormy skies, her halo of curly, wispy blonde hair framing her face perfectly.

One time, when I was in high school, I went on a class trip to some fancy art museum in Washington, DC, and I can perfectly recall this beautiful painting of some royal princess with a shock of blonde ringlets and an eerily wise, knowing expression on her face. I've always thought Dakota looks just like that princess from the painting. Sometimes I just look at her and have to do a double take, thinking about how wild it is that I managed to produce such a lovely, angelic child. Who knew my genetics could ever culminate with a work of art like my little Kota?

Right now, though, my tiny masterpiece is staring at me expectantly, and I remember that I've been summoned into this room to stop the ultimate crime from continuing. So I pat Kota on her chubby cheek and walk over to kneel down on the rug beside the two boys, Grant and Weston. The two of them are so engrossed in their own works of art (a purple rhinoceros or perhaps a dinosaur and a three-story house with what looks like an apple tree out front, respectively), that they don't even look up at me at first. But then I clear my throat and they seem to be shaken back to reality, blinking up at my face blankly.

I give them my most charitable smile and say softly, "Could you boys do me a favor?"

Grant just starts to pick his nose while staring right into my face, but Weston answers in a sweet voice, "Uh-huh. Sure, Miss Crystal. What is it?"

I pick up the broken crayons and hold them out for them to see. "I would really like it if you would stop snapping the crayons in half. It's no fun coloring with broken crayons, right?" I suggest. Dakota is leaning over my shoulder now, staring the boys down like she's the bad cop and I'm the good cop. That's my girl.

"But if I break the blue one in half, that means

Grant can use blue at the same time as me," Weston points out. Grant nods.

"Then there's two blues," the other little boy agrees.

Dakota says, "But...but you can't break things. It's against the *law*."

It takes every ounce of my restraint not to burst out laughing at my daughter's indignation, especially because I can kind of understand the boys' logic here. They're not breaking the crayons to be annoying. They're doing it to be able to share more effectively. This is yet another one of the millions of conundrums I encounter regarding my job every day. Kids are way smarter and more contemplative than anyone seems to suspect from them. Most of the time, it's my job here to guide them away from the dumb (but logical to them) decisions they make. But then other times, like this, all I can really do is just nod and try to see it their way.

"Alright. You have a good point, boys. I guess you can break them once in half. But don't break the halves into smaller pieces, okay? Because then it will be too hard to hold, and what's the use of a crayon you can't even hold onto?" I tell them, smiling warmly.

Grant and Weston look pleased that I've approved their system, but I can feel Kota positively squirming with annoyance, so I pre-emptively take her by the hand and lead her out of the room and toward the kitchen, hoping to distract her by asking her to help me out with breakfast for the group.

Apart from the two boys who are both five years old and will be starting kindergarten in a few weeks, there's also another little girl named Hailey who is three. She's currently conked out on the pink sofa, her arms wrapped around her favorite stuffed whale toy she lovingly refers to as "Whailey." Hailey and Whailey are virtually inseparable. One time, her mother, who is a single parent with a demanding paralegal job, accidentally forgot to bring Whailey with them to drop Hailey off here and the little girl screamed for approximately two straight hours because it upset her so much. So nowadays, we kind of treat Whailey like a VIP. As long as she's got him to snuggle, Hailey is perfectly well-behaved, even when she gets cranky at nap time.

And when there are anywhere from four to eight small children in my house at any given time during the work day, I'll take whatever possible forms of relief I can get. If that means treating a stuffed animal like it's a human person who gets to sit in a high chair at the table with the rest of the actual living, breathing kids, then so be it.

"Why you let them keep breakin' my colors?" asks Dakota as we walk into the kitchen together. She's blinking up at me, those green eyes etched with confusion and a hint of betrayal. Poor kid. I hate seeing that look on her face, like I've let her down. But I try to remind myself that part of being a mom is just that: teaching the tiny person you love more than anything else in the world that sometimes, life is not totally fair, and sometimes you have to put up with crap you don't like. So I scoop her up into my arms and hoist her onto the kitchen counter, leaning in to kiss her on the forehead. She blanches and giggles, trying to squirm away unsuccessfully.

"I mean it, Mommy. Why?" she persists.

"Boy, you're one stubborn little girl, aren't you?" I laugh, shaking my head. "They were trying to share better, and you know that sharing is very important. They weren't doing it to hurt you, but to help each other. Do you understand?"

"But they'll be too tiny to color with!"

"Well, don't worry about the crayons, sweetheart. If they get too broken up to use, I'll buy you some more. I promise I will."

"Pinky promise?" she pipes up, defiantly sticking out her little chin. I grin at her, my heart near to exploding with pure love for this pint-sized negotiator.

I hold out my pinky for her to link up with her own tiny pinky finger. I raise our laced fingers to my lips for a kiss and declare, "Pinky promise."

Kota smiles broadly, showing the first loose tooth she's ever had, the center bottom left. At first, when she started noticing how wobbly it was, I panicked, thinking that she was way too young for a loose tooth. It seems like just yesterday that she grew all those cute little baby teeth to begin with. But after several frantic calls to the pediatrician and the dentist (and my mom, who lives across town), I have been assured that it's within normal age range for a loose tooth. A little early, but nothing to worry about.

Of course, that doesn't do much to stop me from worrying anyway. That's kind of part and parcel of being a mother: you worry. All the time. About everything. Whether it's warranted or not. But by now, I've kind of learned how to just cope with the constant concern. It's mostly just background noise in my brain at this point, and it rarely keeps me from fully enjoying myself in the moment.

Like right now, as I hand Kota a jar of peanut butter and a spoon. Watching her carefully, I let her help make the sandwiches by globbing a spoonful of creamy peanut butter onto each pair of bread slices. I use a butter knife to spread it, of course, but I like giving her the opportunity to feel helpful, even if I don't feel safe letting her handle the knife herself just yet.

"Good job, Kota," I tell her. "That's a pretty even distribution of PB you got there."

"Thanks, Mommy. I'm pretty good at peanut butter," she agrees proudly.

I giggle. "Yes, you are. Very talented."

I quickly finish making the peanut-butter-and-banana sandwiches for the children, plating them up with some sliced peaches and a small handful of graham crackers shaped like bunnies. Some mornings, I'll test out different recipes like cheesy scrambled eggs with sourdough toast, fruit salad with little triangles of cheddar cheese on the side, or even maybe an eggy, veggie-filled quiche if I'm feeling especially adventurous. But to be honest, the vast majority of the time, these kids would rather just eat something simple and unpretentious. Still, I do my best to introduce new foods to them, partly because I think it broadens their horizons just a pinch and partly because, well, I just really enjoy cooking. And sometimes I want to make something a little less pedestrian than a PB-and-J.

"You ready to eat?" I ask Dakota. She nods vigorously, her green eyes round with glee. I help her down from the counter and she takes off running full-tilt down the hallway to the playroom while I follow after her, balancing four little plates on my arms.

I'm thankful to have this skill, which I developed as a teenager when I worked at the golf course across town. I was a waitress at the lounge club back then, and it was a job I continued for a while after Kota was born. Back then, I was desperate for money and stability. I was only eighteen when she was born, and I was in way over my head. The father of my child has never been a part of her life. It's not his fault. He was destined for greatness, and by the time I found out I was pregnant...

I shake the thought from my head. I'm grateful for the experience of raising her. It made me learn how to be self-sufficient. Once I saved up enough money from my waitressing tips to move out of my parents' tiny bungalow and get my own little town-house just a few miles from the beach, I quit my job at the golf course to start up this daycare instead. I've taken a lot of certificate classes on childcare, safety, and first aid, so I'm pretty well-qualified for my current career. It's not the most lucrative living, of course, and I'm still making a whole lot less money than the big spenders, retired folks, and tourists who blow through the Outer Banks, where I live, all the time. But I get by. And as a middle-class, young, single, unwed mother in Kitty Hawk, North Carolina, that's pretty good.

I set down the plates for the kids to eat, and they all excitedly dig in. Content that they'll be safe and well-behaved for a few minutes while they're stuffing their faces, I duck away to the living room, where the TV is still playing the local news. I sit down on the edge of the couch to nibble some graham cracker bunnies while I catch up on current events. I don't get a whole lot of time to myself in this job, so I've learned to snatch a couple minutes here and there whenever possible. I watch as the newscaster announces that it's time for the weather.

"Ugh. The boring part," I mumble to myself, leaning back against the cushion. "It's already raining out, I know. What more can you tell me?"

But to my surprise, the usually-chipper weather guy is wearing more than just his typical brightly-patterned tie (this time, it's a pink-and-teal flamingo print). There is also a rather wary expression on his handsome face as he explains that perhaps this is more than just your everyday, normal bout of rainfall on the drizzly east coast. He seems to be staring right at me through the TV screen when he explains, "Those of us out here in the Outer Banks— Kitty Hawk and Kill Devil Hills— keep an eye out for a possible heavy rainfall and storm conditions as the newly-christened Tropical Storm Bruno makes its way across the Atlantic. Here at the meteorologists' station, we are not very concerned at the moment, as it looks like the storm may peter out before landing on our beautiful shores, but stay tuned for updates, just in case."

"Can't believe flights haven't been cancelled yet," I hear another passenger say behind me as I make my way off the plane, breathing in the familiar North Carolina air.

"We got lucky. Bruno is getting stronger out there. Might have landed just in time for a storm party."

Bruno is the name of the tropical storm brewing just off the coast. I heard about it before I even got on the plane to head over here. But even if it had been a full-blown hurricane, it couldn't have stopped me from getting here. Nothing could have.

I'm home.

This airport is small compared to a lot of the ones I've flown through over the years, and it's always strange stepping back into the civilian world. In the military, everything is regimented. That only changed ever so slightly as I climbed my way through the ranks to become a SEAL. With the higher prestige came more freedom when it came to things like this— deciding when I could take some personal time.

As far as I was concerned, Tropical Storm Bruno was just another excuse to add onto the pile of excuses to suddenly decide to head to the Outer Banks of North Carolina for a few weeks.

Kitty Hawk is more than just my hometown. Plenty of people I went through training with want nothing to do with their hometown, some for better reasons than others. But me, I've always taken pride in the strip of islands off the eastern coast of North Carolina. Having been all over the world, I feel like I can say with some confidence that it's one of the most beautiful places on earth.

I'm only a little biased.

That was more than enough for my executive officer to give me leave. I'm usually a modest man, but I've busted my ass the past year, flying from country to country dealing with some of the worst crime lords the world has to offer, and it has paid off with the men who decide where I go and when. In short, I have leverage, and I'm using it for something important to me.

I head into the bathroom to wash my face off. It's my ritual when I get off a plane— I have to wash off the stale air and feel fresh, like a new day starting wherever I go. I'd never tell my comrades that's why I do it, of course. I look myself in the mirror after drying off the cool water and take a deep breath.

I'm twenty-two and standing in my hometown all over again. I look so different, in my eyes. I've seen so much since I left here as a fresh-faced high school graduate four years ago. I've saved lives and taken them, usually in the same hour. I've diffused bombs and put bullets in the hearts of some of the most evil men I could have dreamed of. Sometimes, it still doesn't feel real.

Will she see the same guy she fell for all those years ago?

Crystal.

That name has been in the back of my mind ever since I left. Hell, I left so soon after graduating that I'll be amazed if she even recognizes me.

Especially since she doesn't know I'm here.

A lot of complicated feelings are racing through my heart right now. I head out of the airport and see the gorgeous Carolina skies above me as I head over to the car rental office. Familiar birds soaring over-head, familiar scents in the air, it all comes rushing back to me all at once. It's like I never left.

But that's not the reality. This place has changed since I went away. The people have moved on with their lives, especially the ones I was close to when I graduated high school and signed up for the Navy. Four years is just a flash in the pan for people in their later years, but between now and high school, people can change entirely.

I wonder how Crystal has changed.

That thought haunts me. I know I still have to see her, in one capacity or another.

It was a wild idea that came to me in the jungle that brought me here. Sitting there in a barely-dry shelter in pitch-black night time listening to strange animals rustle around me, I imagined what things might have been like if I'd never left. I pictured Crystal and I driving across the country, maybe a little road trip through the South, hopping from restaurant to restaurant and sightseeing like a couple of tourists.

Knowing what kind of man I've become, that thought is almost funny. But I found myself dwelling on it. So, I decided that if all went well on the last mission, I'd stop by home and check in.

I just couldn't leave Crystal with nothing more than the last night we spent together.

It had been a high school graduation party. It seems so juvenile now, but back then, we were on top of the world, our whole lives ahead of us. It was exciting and terrifying at the same time. I knew what I wanted to do— and I did it. But that didn't blunt the sting of what it felt like to leave everything behind. Crystal was one of those things that hurt the most to leave.

The feeling of having her in bed that last night at

the party has stuck with me for four long years. It was more than just sex, so much more. I felt closer to her in that moment than ever in my life, with anyone. It was such a strong bond that I almost entertained the idea of backing out of the Navy and taking a job locally for a little while longer to see where things might go.

Dwelling on one night together wasn't good, so I didn't obsess over it, but it was always there for me to think about when the nights were blackest. And out in the wilderness, wherever that may be... God, the nights do get black. Strong as I am, I'm still human.

A few minutes later, the rental car manager, and older man, is handing me a set of keys to a mid-size SUV and giving me a firm nod.

"Drive safe out there," he says. "The news is saying this will be a modest tropical storm, but I've seen a few in my life, and I know when it feels worse in the air than they're making it sound."

"I hear you," I say, nodding. "Think it'll cause any damage?"

"Well, what doesn't get damaged out here when a storm hits?" he says with a chuckle. "We're one big storm barrier."

"Yeah, we are, aren't we?" I admit with a soft laugh.

"You from around here? I thought I recognized that accent."

"Born and raised," I say.

"Well, welcome back!" he says, shaking my hand. "And thank you for your service."

Driving down the road, I can tell he wasn't kidding about the storm. The skies are getting darker, and the trees are billowing a hell of a lot more ominously than the news made it sound. It puts a dark tinge over what's otherwise a jarring drive down memory lane.

I see the old doughnut shop I used to visit, and the same owner is getting a couple employees to help him board up the windows. A convenience store I used a lot is putting up signs saying they're out of gasoline. Old restaurants I used to hang out at are closing early.

We're part of a strip of islands here, so it's easy for bad weather to hit us hard, but this is surprising. I start to wonder about Crystal.

I checked in on her social media before I came to visit, of course. I didn't do it to stalk her, obviously, but just to make sure she wasn't married or seeing someone or moved away. Unfortunately, she doesn't have much of a presence. Her mom posted on her page asking if she could borrow some eggs, though, so I know that she's still living in Kitty Hawk, and the phonebook gave me her address. I figured, if there's a bad storm brewing, though, she might need some help. Or at least, that'll be my excuse for showing up out of the blue.

I turn on the radio in the car as I drive past a growing stream of cars headed in the opposite direction and listen to the voice crackling through it.

". . . motorists should be advised that the 64 bridge is now closed, as Tropical Storm Bruno has been upgraded to a category-2 hurricane. Meteorologists are actively tracking the storm's alarming growth, and a statement will soon be made regarding the safety of remaining on the Outer Bank for the duration of the storm. Residents are advised to take the usual safety precautions seriously: boarding up windows and clearing yards of debris is strongly advised."

I furrow my brow. This is starting to sound like more than just something worthy of a cozy storm party night indoors, and the further I drive, it's starting to look like a lot more than that, too.

The road takes me close to the beach on the east side, and I turn my head to look out to the waves. I can tell the water is angry. I've spent a lot of time out on those shores. I drank out here illegally with the other boys as a teenager, and I played out here endless afternoons as a kid.

I'm not some kind of hippie, but water has a spirit to it, anywhere you go. The Atlantic coast has it just as much as the Amazon river has it. When you get to know the water, you can sense when something's not right.

And I've got a bad feeling in the pit of my stomach.

"Traffic onto the Outer Banks has now been suspended, including the 158 bridge. We now have a statement from First Flight Airport regarding the incoming storm: all incoming flights are being redirected to the nearest available airports, and all departures are suspended until the end of the storm. If possible, residents are encouraged to evacuate to the mainland safely. Coast Guard personnel are en route to the 158 bridge to ensure safe evacuation in lieu of Hurricane Bruno's projected upgrade to a category-4 hurricane within the next hour."

My eyes widen as I look down at the radio, then back up to the crackle of lightning out to the east. I clench my jaw.

There's a hell of a storm out there, and it's getting bigger...fast.

CRYSTAL

 sit in front of the television in the living room, perched on the edge of the couch cushion with my eyes wide and my chin resting on my knee, which is folded up to my chest while the other dangles off the couch. Ever since I was a little girl, this has been the way I sit when I'm anxious.

Years and years ago, nearly a decade now, I sat just like this in the waiting room of the nearby hospital while awaiting the inevitable bad news from the medical staff tasked with looking after my father. Back then, I was just a skinny, gawky twelve year old with no idea how the world worked and certainly no idea that my world would continue spinning on its axis once the doctors informed my mother and me that he was gone.

But after all the shock and the tears and the "how do we make a life without Dad in it," I was left with the same advice I received from the man himself all throughout my childhood: *find a way to make it through, and then find a way to make it good.*

That has been the motto I've worn like a backbone for years and years, and while it has been very difficult at times to follow it, and even more difficult to believe in it, I have to admit that Dad knew what he was talking about.

When I got pregnant with Dakota, I was just eighteen years old. I had just graduated from high school and my plan at the time was to go to university to get my teaching degree. My father used to teach third grade—I even got the uniquely weird experience of being his student for that grade—so I was determined to follow in his footsteps.

Besides, I have always been pretty good with children. They listen to me and seem to bond with me very quickly. I love kids. Even with as unpredictable as they can be sometimes, especially around certain ages, I love the honesty and earnestness with which they seem to view the world around them. Everything is new. Everything is interesting. Even the most mundane of routines can look like an adventure from the eyes of a child.

Sometimes, when I'm feeling bored and bogged down by the dull monotony of daily life, all I have to do is listen to my daughter talk about her day and suddenly the universe brightens up a little. She sees things I overlook, finds joy in the tiny minutiae that slip right past me. It's truly a blessing to have her alongside me as a copilot for life.

That's not to say I didn't panic when I found out I was pregnant with her.

I mean, I was just a bright-eyed, naive, optimistic eighteen-year-old with a game plan that was now being totally rerouted...and I didn't even know the new destination yet. I was just scrambling to get some semblance of my life together, still waiting tables at the golf club, sending off college applications even though I knew I probably couldn't handle going to school full-time while working full-time *and* being a new mom. One of the three had to go.

Obviously, Dakota was not going anywhere. And I needed that job to pay my bills and to slip into my savings account if I wanted to ever have a shot at moving out and living independently from my mother.

So it was the university degree that got sidelined. Now, I look back and realize that was the best possible decision I could have made at the time, but back then? Well, let's just say I spent a lot of long hours in the evenings after work, perched on my bed with one knee up and one leg hanging, my usual panic-pose.

The same position I'm sitting in right now as the news channel flashes back and forth from boring local stories to the coverage of Tropical Storm Bruno.

The reason I am so anxious about it is that I can hear, see, *and* feel this storm already. The air is tight, the thunder rumbling overhead sounds like the deep growls of some humongous ancient beast, and the rain is falling so hard that my little potted plants on the back patio have probably drowned by now.

Now, here's the thing: the folks living here in the Outer Banks of North Carolina are no strangers to stormy weather. That's part and parcel of living on the east coast, on a conglomeration of barrier islands. Kitty Hawk, the small seaside tourist town I have been an inhabitant of for my entire twenty-two years of life, buckles down and prepares for hurricane season around the same time every single year.

We all go to the grocery store weeks ahead of time to stock up on giant crates of bottled waters, canned goods, dry foods that don't have to be cooked just in case the power goes out. Everyone I know has a small stockpile of candles, flashlights, and batteries.

When you live on the edge of the world like we do, you get used to some pretty dodgy weather. In the summers, we are lucky to get a lot of sunny beach days. That's the good part. And in the winter, the temperatures never drop too low. That's a good part, too.

But hurricane season is the trade-off. That's the

price we pay for life on the beach. Still, we are a hardy and sensible population, and we generally don't lose our minds over a little rain and lightning. We don't close our schools or cancel the workday for a little precipitation.

But this...I can feel this time is different somehow.

I know I should probably remain calm. I mean, I have been keeping an eye on the news channel all morning just in case the weather guy tells me it's time to freak out. Normally, if there's a hurricane brewing somewhere out on the Atlantic, our meteorologist can predict it way ahead of time. Hours, even days before it will ever make landfall.

We take a note of the impending horror, make the necessary adjustments to schedules, plans, what have you. We make sure our usual hurricane supplies aren't dwindling, and we top up whatever might be lacking. It's gotten to the point now where we don't really have to panic. It's all to be expected, and the science of weather-predicting has been sharpened to a fine point, so I trust what the weather guy says.

The powers that be christened the storm Tropical Storm Bruno. Not Hurricane Bruno. Just another tropical storm to blow crazy gusts that sound like the wailing of monsters through the palm trees, pour down enough rain to cause some light flooding, maybe even close down a few minor roadways. A tropical storm, back when I was growing up, often just meant I had a built-in excuse to stay indoors and dive into an especially juicy e-book, just while away the hours engrossed in a story.

And sometimes, the approaching maelstrom will cool off and calm down long before it even reaches our shores, to be downgraded to just another run-of-the-mill thunderstorm. No need to worry. I expected that to happen this time.

After all, if it is a real and present threat to our safety, wouldn't the news let us know?

If I have reason to worry, surely the weather man would have made that clear by now. He has never let me down before, to my memory. I can't remember a time when a tropical storm snowballed out of control to become more dangerous than predicted. And yet, I just have a feeling in my gut warning me that something isn't quite right.

So I am sitting here totally transfixed, my eyes on the television screen while the cogs of my mind turn faster and faster, picking up anxiety as they circulate. An ad for some kind of luxurious body wash comes on the screen and I roll my eyes, wishing the commercial break would end so I can get back to the weather updates.

Just as I'm about to get up and go grab a second mug of coffee while I'm waiting, a massive clap of thunder cracks through the sky directly overhead. It is so loud that it makes me yelp in genuine terror, and I feel the power of the thunder vibrate my whole house.

Uh oh.

That pit in my stomach is getting heavier by the second, and my heart pounds wildly in my chest as I hear the kids from the next room cry out, clearly terrified by the thunder. I leap off the couch and go bolting into the playroom, fully prepared to go into comfort mode. When I round the corner, I almost run smack into Kota, who apparently came running for me.

"Mommy! Big thunder! It was so loud!" she whimpers, her sweet little face contorted with tearful fright. Her eyes look even deeper green with the tears shimmering in them.

"Oh, honey, I know. It was scary, huh?" I coo, immediately kneeling down to sweep her up into my arms. She throws her pudgy arms around my neck and buries her face in my shoulder, trembling like a Chihuahua in the rain. I stroke her curly blonde hair and stand up to go into the playroom to check on the children. If Dakota is scared, the others must be, too.

When I step into the room, I'm surprised to find all three of the little ones standing by the window, peering out at the stormy skies. The rain is slamming into the windowpane so hard that it's difficult to see out and get a good glimpse of how bad it is out there. I hurry over to the window and start trying to shoo them away toward the couch, as I know from my own childhood that it's more dangerous to stand by a window during a storm of this caliber.

"Come on, kids, away from the window now," I chide them gently, reaching down with my free hand to guide them back away. Grant looks up at me with huge, round eyes full of wonder and fear. I can see the tears just slightly starting to shimmer there, making his gaze look glossy and shiny.

"It's rainin' a lot," he murmurs, a little breathlessly. My heart aches for the little guy as he tries to make sense of the storm.

I nod at him and manage to summon up a smile. "I know. It's really loud, isn't it? But don't worry. We're safe inside," I assure him, ruffling his brown hair with my free hand.

"Are you sure?" Hailey asks in the tiniest, most frightened little voice. I look down at her to see that she's sucking her thumb and she's got her trusty stuffed whale, Whailey, tucked under her arm as usual. For some reason, her question strikes fear deep into my soul.

I know why. It's because I'm *not* sure. I'm not sure that we'll be okay. Because when I look out the window, the world outside is dark. Way, way too dark for half past noon on a summer's day. It looks like night is falling, like the sun has been sucked up into a black hole, leaving us shrouded in darkness as the rain pours heavily.

"Yes, sweetheart. I'm going to keep you all safe, okay? Got it?" I assure them with as much confidence as I can muster. Grant, Weston, and Hailey all crowd around me, wrapping their little arms around my legs and waist.

"Come on, let's go in the other room so I can watch the weather man, alright?" I tell them, leading them out of the playroom and into the adjoining living room. The commercial break has ended by now, and as soon as we walk into the room, I see the local news station flash over to the weather.

This time, the meteorologist looks downright freaked out. That cannot be a good sign of things to come. The kids pile onto the sofa with me, Whailey and all. I snuggle them close as I listen to the weather guy, my heart thumping like crazy with every word out of his mouth.

"Folks, it looks like we might have counted our chickens before they hatched," he admits with a deeply furrowed brow. "Tropical Storm Bruno has hit a warm patch and is now being upgraded to a hurricane. This is all happening very quickly, and I'm here to do my best to keep the good people of the Outer Banks updated on what to do and where to go in case of... well, if the worst happens."

"The worst?" Weston repeats nervously. I reach over and give his thin shoulder a squeeze. He grabs a pillow from the end of the couch and hugs it close to his chest, cuddling up closer to Grant. I'm grateful that the kids I watch all get along so well. Especially in a time like this, when the shit appears to really, truly be hitting the fan.

"The local police are in the process of closing all but major thoroughfares right now," says the weather man. "Businesses are shutting down for the day so that employees can go home in time to prep for the hurricane. The timeline we here at the meteorology station established earlier this morning is being accelerated to fit the new conditions caused by Hurricane Bruno. I have just received word that evacuation centers are being set up to help get folks out of dodge. Again, I want to apologize for how quickly things have changed. I have to admit, we— we did not see this coming."

"Shit," I murmur aloud as my blood runs cold.

All four kids gasp. Dakota frowns and says, "That's a bad word."

"Yes. Yes, it is, sweetie. I'm sorry. Don't repeat that word— any of you," I reply hastily. "I, uh, I should make some phone calls and see if I can get a hold of your parents," I tell the other kids as I fumble around in my pocket for my phone. I slide the screen open and select my contacts list, deciding to start with Hailey's mom. I dial her number and press the phone against my ear. It rings only twice before Hailey's mother, Katherine, picks up.

"Hi, Kat? Are you there?" I ask into the phone receiver.

All I get in response are some garbled words, the service dipping in and out so badly that I can't even put the sounds together to make sense of them. "Hello?" I ask again, frowning. Once again, the audio clips in and out, and I can't tell whether she's even on the other end of the line or not. The storm must be messing with the cell towers somehow. Just as I'm about to say something else, the line cuts out.

I stare at the phone blankly for a moment before realizing the kids are all watching me and I need to maintain a brave face. So I quickly move down the contacts list to call Grant's dad instead. I get the same spotty service before the line cuts out. Starting to panic, I try Weston's mom next, only to receive more of the same. By now, I'm starting to feel sick to my stomach. I don't know what to do. I can't reach their parents. I have no idea if they're still stuck at work or if they're in traffic trying to get here to collect their children before evacuation. I don't know if maybe they've already been forced to go to the evacuation centers sans children. If the police are blocking the roads already… well, then things must be pretty serious.

And there's no way I can evacuate. Not with these four small children. Not with the winds howling and the rain pelting down like a biblical flood. Not with the lightning cracking the dark sky into flashes of searing hot light and the thunder shaking the earth. It isn't safe for us to leave the house. All I can do is bunker down with these four tiny innocents and hope against hope that the hurricane doesn't plow us down in its path.

Just as I'm contemplating how screwed I am, another clap of powerful thunder— even closer than before— cracks through the silence and makes us all scream out in fear.

"Mommy! I'm scared!" Dakota cries out, clinging to me tightly.

"I want my daddy!" Weston whimpers.

Grant and Hailey both begin to cry, clearly traumatized by the storm. I can't sit here any longer. We're too close to the window. I hurriedly get to my feet and scoop Hailey up onto my left hip and Dakota onto my right, then gesture for the boys, who are slightly bigger and older, to follow me as I rush through the trembling townhouse to the most interior room: the bathroom.

"Come on! Let's go!" I command, leading them into the tiny bathroom and shutting the door. "Into the tub, all of you."

I cradle Dakota and Hailey against my chest as I hunker down in the bathtub, helping Weston and Grant climb over the side to sit down squished up next to us. I yank the shower curtain closed, as if that could possibly help protect us in some way, and start doing my best to comfort the little ones. But they're all so terrified that they're inconsolable, crying and shaking as they cling to me for dear life.

I'm fighting tears of my own, wishing I had some better plan, some way of sparing these little angels from the trauma of the hurricane. I only hope we can ride it out safely here. But no sooner has this thought crossed my mind than another gigantic, earth-shattering blast of thunder rumbles through the house down to the very foundation...and all the lights go out.

*A*drenaline surges through my body as the clap of thunder shatters the air around me, a bolt of lightning bigger than anything I've ever seen crackling onto the telephone pole just a few feet ahead of me off to the left side of the road. I slam on the brakes and skid to try to avoid the falling power lines. Sparks flare up all around the road as the power goes out in what I imagine must be half of the town, if not more.

My ears are still ringing from the thunderclap by the time my SUV comes to a halt. I hear static on the radio, and now there's a pole in the middle of the road. The last thing the radio told me was that Bruno has been upgraded to a cat-5.

This is insane. Part of me wonders if I'm dreaming, and this is some kind of worst-case-scenario nightmare playing out in front of my eyes. Over the past few minutes, I've passed a handful of cars flying by me way faster than they should be going in a situation like this, all desperate to evacuate as fast as possible. The skies are nearly black now, casting such a strange lighting over everything that doesn't help the feeling of everything being surreal.

I've seen bad storms before. Hell, I've lived through monsoons with nothing but the gear on my back to deal with them. But I've never seen anything like this. Worse, the town is obviously nowhere near ready to deal with a catastrophe of this magnitude. Under reporting disasters costs lives more often than people realize, and the more time I spend driving through this nightmare, the more I'm realizing that might just be what I'm dealing with today.

I feel my training starting to kick in. Regardless of whether or not I'm on leave, I'm still a SEAL. If there's anyone equipped to handle a situation like this, it's me. And if I weren't on my way to pick up a girl who might just be in danger, I'd be going door to door right now, making sure the people have or are in the process of evacuating.

I take a deep breath and look to the road. The wires are strewn across it haphazardly, but it isn't safe to handle them right now. I turn my SUV and pull off the road, onto the sandy grass and toward someone's yard. The place has no garage and no cars out front, so I can only imagine the occupants already left. At least, that's what I have to tell myself to feel okay just pulling around their backyard to get around the wreckage in the road.

Luck isn't on my side today, though. As soon as I get around the house, I see that the damage is already starting. Someone's trampoline has been blown into the yard, leaning against shattered windows on the back porch. There are also large branches lying around, which tell me its only a matter of time before I start seeing entire trees in the same state.

Instead of awkwardly trying to drive this thing around what I see to be a smashed fence on the side of the yard, I pull through to the neighborhood on the opposite side. I'll take my chances in the suburbs instead of hoping that was the only piece of electrified debris lying in the main road that stretches up and down the Outer Banks.

The neighborhood I drive into isn't in a much better state, though. I pull out onto the narrow streets to see several garbage cans strewn around, all apparently full to bursting when the wind dealt with them. Figures something like this would happen on garbage day.

Despite the debris everywhere, my SUV manages to hold its own as I wade through the neighborhood. I start thinking about what route to take, since the main road isn't my best option. As I'm thinking about that, though, some sudden movement from one of the houses gets my attention. It's a woman, waving her arms and clearly trying to flag me down as I drive by slowly. I'm suspicious at first, but then I recognize the face—it's a woman named Anne, someone who was in my graduating class. She was always a tough woman back then, always head of whatever sports team she joined up with, and she joined as many as she could.

If there was anyone who would feel safe running up to a potentially dangerous stranger in an unfamiliar car in the middle of a storm, it was probably her. That didn't make the look on her face when I rolled the window down any less priceless.

"Holy shit, Duncan?!" she blurts, eyes wide.

"Little windy to be out for a walk, isn't it?" I joke. I've always found that dumb jokes take the sting out of dire situations like this.

"Shut the fuck up," she says, laughing despite herself. "What the hell are you doing out here? Did the military send you as part of the evacuation plan?"

"I wish I could say so," I reply, frowning. "I'm on leave. Might have been on the last flight in before they started redirecting them. What the hell is all this? Why weren't people prepared?"

"This is unheard of!" she blurts. "It was supposed to be just a regular storm, not the fucking apocalypse! Nobody was expecting this, not even the news. I ran out here thinking you were a tourist heading back to the mainland. I was about to try to get a ride back with you."

"Where's your car?"

"My husband has it. He works on the other side of the bridge, and it got closed before he had a chance to get over here. Traffic on the mainland is swamped with people trying to get to their stranded relatives, apparently. You're not heading back that way, are you? Don't take this the wrong way, but a Marine or whatever you are is probably the best kind of person to get a ride from in a storm like this."

I could correct her, but that will have to wait wait.

"Actually, I was headed the opposite direction," I say. "Do you know if Crystal is out and safe?"

"Ahhh, so that's why you're here," she says, putting her hands on her hips. "Should have known not even the military could keep you two apart, Romeo. Hate to be the bearer of bad news, but the roads further down toward her house are closed. There are power lines down and someone's boat in the middle of the road."

"Shit!" I think for a moment, frowning. "Wait, she runs a daycare, doesn't she?" Or at least there's a daycare operating out of her home address, according to the phone book. "Are there still kids down there?"

"We don't keep in touch these days, but it's the

middle of a week day," she says, confirming my fears. If the roads closed down this fast, then a lot of parents probably didn't have a chance to get their kids home safely. That also means that Crystal is definitely still down there, through roads that a car can't pass through. My mind races. I need to get to Crystal, but I can't just let people in need stay behind when I could help them, either.

"Her place is normally another five minute drive from here, isn't it?"

"That sounds right," she answers.

"Take my car," I say, and she stares at me, stunned.

"Like...just take it? What do you mean?"

"Take my car and drive it to the Coast Guard blockade on the bridge," I say firmly, my plan coming together in my head. "I can't get where I need to go by car, anyway. I'll go on foot and use Crystal's car to get the kids when I get there. I'm not going to leave you stranded here, but I can't just turn around and abandon Crystal either."

She opens her mouth to protest, but another thunderclap overhead makes her jump.

"Fine, fine— is this your car?"

"Rental, so don't worry about damage. I'd be surprised if you can make it back to the bridge without a little wear and tear," I add with a smirk.

"Smartass," she says as I get out of the car with

my single backpack to let her climb into the driver's seat. "Are you sure about this?"

"Am I the type to second guess myself?"

"Fair," she sighs. "Take care of Crystal, okay?"

"Avoid the main road and stay safe," I say, patting the hood of the car. She nods, pulls off, and I watch her disappear around the same yard I cut across to get here. Now, it's just me, my backpack, and all the distance between here and Crystal.

Five minutes in a car along mostly straight roads is still a healthy distance on foot, especially in this weather. Hot, humid wind buffets me as I trudge across yards, relying on my memory to get me through the town and neighborhoods I remember so clearly. I hear sirens in the distance, both north and south. Car alarms go off, and I hear a beat of one every now and then.

I'm surprised not to run into as many people on the rest of the trek south. Occasionally, I pass a small family packing things into a car in a hurry and pulling away, but none of them bother me. I'm six and a half feet of muscle wandering around on foot in a hurricane that's about to land— simple common sense tells most people not to bother me. I wouldn't turn anyone away, but I don't mind getting ignored. The sooner I can get to Crystal, the better.

But fate doesn't let me off that easy. After clearing the first neighborhood, rain starts to patter against my skin, and I realize that the first band of Hurricane Bruno is making landfall.

I pass by an opening in the buildings to get a view of the main road, and I see men in uniform by large jeeps with equipment. It must be the Coast Guard. I don't want to engage with them right now, but I make a mental note of where they are on the road. They'll be the closest point of contact.

I take out a windbreaker in my bag and pull it over my shoulders. It won't keep all the rain out, but it's better than just my t-shirt. At least it isn't freezing cold.

I finally make it to the outskirts of the neighborhood where I know Crystal's home is, moving along the outskirts, and the closer I get to the shore, I realize why everything looks slightly off.

Floods. We're used to floods here on this narrow island chain, but not to the point that we can handle flash floods on such short notice like this. It's only going to get worse from here on out, too.

The wind is getting harder. Much harder. The rain is already slanted, but within a few minutes, it's a full-on horizontal downpour that whips me as I try to hike across yards that are starting to squelch underfoot with the rising water. My heart starts pounding in my chest, not because I'm worried about my own safety, but because I keep thinking about how high the water might be by the time I reach Crystal and try to get out of here.

The wind nearly blows me off my feet as I enter the neighborhood proper and start wandering down the streets, following the house numbers. She's around here somewhere close, I know that much. I didn't exactly get a chance to memorize the route, but I know the area well. I used to ride my bike over every inch of the place when I was a kid.

But when I finally do reach the house numbers that are close to where Crystal's should be, my heart sinks. My eyes pan over to a series of townhouses, and I feel building dread as I count the numbers on them...until the colossal tree lying horizontally in front of them blocks the numbers from view.

"Fuck," I curse under my breath, and I take off in a sprint across the road toward the townhouse. There are more trees around here than you might expect, and while none of them are especially huge for trees, a fallen tree can still do a hell of a lot of damage. It doesn't take much to cave a roof in.

I reach the tree and try to pull on it, but it's too heavy from where I am. I start looking up and down the row of townhouses until I find a spot that looks like I can wedge myself into it. I climb over the trunk and put my back against the wall of one of the houses, planting my feet firmly on the trunk. All at once, I make my body's muscles work together to push, channeling every ounce of strength I have.

Inch by inch, the tree starts to budge. It has some traction in the dirt, but I don't care. I'm full of adrenaline and know that Crystal is trapped in there, along with anyone else who got locked in by the tree.

Finally, there's enough room for me to get to the door of Crystal's house. My mind races with horrible images, thinking that she could be unconscious inside, or that a power surge is starting a fire. They're irrational thoughts, but that doesn't matter to me right now. I try the door handle, but it doesn't budge.

Locked.

I knock, and wait, but there's nothing. If she *is* in there, she probably can't hear me over the storm. I slam my fists harder on the door, but still nothing. I can't access any other entrances, and this is the only way to get in.

But I'm not about to let that stop me. Looking around, I find a thick branch on the tree that looks sturdy, but it's already half broken off from the trunk. I brace myself, then bring up my leg and kick the thing hard. I hear it crack, but it doesn't give just yet. Another three hard kicks, and the trunk as thick as my leg comes loose. I rush over to it and break off the twigs around it, and just like that, I have a portable battering ram in my hands.

I get myself ready at the front door, and after counting to three in my head, I bring the thing down on the handle. The door shakes, but it doesn't give. I have to get in there. I can't let Crystal and the children stay here while the world falls apart outside, because they'll soon be taken with it.

I bring my little ram down again, and again, and again, all with that one thought burning in my mind:

Get to Crystal.

CRYSTAL

We are all still huddled up together in the bathtub, the four small children clinging to me like I'm the last remaining life preserver after a shipwreck. It is still completely dark in the house. I can hardly see beyond a few feet in front of me, and even when the lights flicker every now and then, it's not enough to help much. This is possibly the worst imaginable situation for it to be dark like this, because it's not just me here—I am surrounded by four kids, all of whom suffer from a fear of the dark in varying degrees.

Grant is in full meltdown mode. He has a flair for the dramatic, which can be good or bad depending on the situation. I often refer to him as Mr. Moody, because when he's sad, he's devastated, and when he's happy, he's on cloud nine. More than once, his father has dropped him off at the start of the day with a quiet warning about whatever state of mind his theatrical son happens to be in.

I truly believe this kid has displayed the full range of possible human emotions all in the same day before. He's being raised by a workaholic father and a mom who travels out of town for work all the time, jetsetting between the east and west coast nearly every week. His parents do everything they can to stay close by and give Grant as much stability and normalcy as possible, and they make damn decent money between their respective lucrative careers.

Even though he's just a little kid, Grant is already a world traveler. His parents don't just take mini staycations to the nearby shore when they have time off. Nope. Not good enough. They fly out to Cancun, Dublin, London, Paris, Mykonos— all over the world. And they take little Grant along with them most of the time. This kid has a passport book with enough stamps to rival a seasoned adult traveler. As a result, he can speak a little bit of a lot of different languages, and he's got a shockingly mature view of the world.

But that doesn't keep him from being afraid of the new and unknown. Immersion therapy can only go so far. He just simply has an excitable personality, and sometimes that means he gets very freaked out. In fact, right now, poor Grant is whimpering and softly crying, his chubby little hands gripping my own larger hand tightly.

I give him a little squeeze of reassurance, not that it will do much good in the face of a big, scary storm like this one. I have a feeling he can sense my fear, too, and that doesn't make this any easier. But I can't help it: I am scared. For my sake, of course, but mostly for the sake of these tiny humans in my care.

Weston is handling it much more calmly, even though I can feel him trembling. He is doing his best to be strong, I can tell. He's always been that way, ever since he started out at my daycare a couple years ago. Despite the fact that he's small and skinny for his age and he wears a pair of tiny, surprisingly thick glasses, he's my little stoic.

Weston rarely cries or gets overwhelmed by events, but even when he does, he keeps the drama to a minimum. His mother and father are a social worker and a psychiatrist at a mental hospital, respectively. Both high-stress, high-demand jobs. And yet they are the most pleasant, beatific pair I have ever met in my life. They never seem to get overly upset or worried about much of anything, which I greatly admire, as a woman who sometimes cries when I watch an especially heartwarming Christmas commercial.

I can only imagine that Weston gets his even-keeled temperament from his peaceful parents. His genetics must be pretty damn solid, psychologically.

His ability to stay relatively chilled-out under duress definitely more than makes up for his unfortunate crappy vision if you ask me.

It's a real breeze caring for a child who rarely cries and never throws a tantrum. Even when he was Hailey's age, he was like a small, well-adjusted grown-up. One time a couple weeks ago we even managed to carry on a strangely mature conversation about paying bills and filing taxes. Sure, he didn't have a whole lot of information to bring to the table on that, considering the fact that he is, indeed, five years old. But he nodded along and seemed to genuinely retain the excruciatingly boring tips I gave him.

As if he would need to know what a W-2 form is anytime soon.

Again, the kid is only five. He's starting kindergarten in a few weeks. But he asked what grown-ups spend their money on, and I couldn't *not* tell him, right? I fully expect this kiddo to become some celebrated, super-rich tech genius when he grows up. At this rate, nothing would shock me. He's a good kid. I know he's holding in his tears and trying to be tough, but I reach over to pat the back of his ginger head, stroking his soft hair in an attempt to comfort him just the same, even though he can't see me.

Hailey, the youngest and most babyish of the four, is now curled up in my lap, resting her little head against my chest. She's sucking her thumb, whimpering in fear every now and then, but overall she is strangely quiet. I think she's in shock, too overwhelmed and stunned by the newness and scariness of our current situation to even react much.

She's going into self-protection mode.

I remember doing that as a little girl, myself.

One summer when I was eight years old, my parents had painstakingly saved up enough money to take us on a family trip to Florida so we could go to Disney World. I was beyond excited, of course, chattering ecstatically about all the fun amusement park rides I was going to go on until it was time to board the airplane for my first flight ever. Something about the claustrophobic airplane cabin, the roar of the engine, the closeness of the other passengers— it sent me into a panic.

But I was eight, and therefore too old to scream and cry. Instead, I just curled up in my seat and stared, petrified, out the window at the clouds drifting by for the duration of the journey. That's what Hailey seems to be doing now. She's retreating into herself, just trying to push out all the scary stuff and hide in a safe space. Her tufty, silky brown hair tickles the underside of my chin as she breathes in and out, and it hurts my heart to feel her own thumping so quickly. She reminds me of a hummingbird—so tiny and delicate. I kiss her on the top of her soft head, hoping that she won't end up too mentally scarred by the hurricane.

And then there's my own daughter, Dakota, who is strangely (and fortunately for me) pretty tough for a three-year-old. She can handle the dark as long as there's a night light plugged in somewhere that can penetrate the darkness a little bit. She is fiercely independent and a self-starter, the kind of child who prefers to figure things out for herself, even if it takes her three times as long as it would with my guidance.

My daughter would rather try something a hundred times by herself and fail miserably on every attempt before ever asking for help, though sometimes I can prod her to accept my assistance before it gets to that point.

When she was a toddler, just learning how to clumsily waddle around the house in nothing but a t-shirt and a pull-up training diaper, she used to bump into things all the time and fall down. Without fail, I would panic and rush over to pick her up, cooing and gushing over my little angel, terrified that she would be badly injured or traumatized by her fall. I was perfectly willing to just cart her around on my hip all day long, never setting her down long enough for her to learn how to do it herself. But she would calmly push my arms away, refusing to be picked up. She doesn't want to be carried, and she certainly does not want to be coddled— she wants to do things on her own.

Dakota is my first and only child, so for the first

year or so of her life I was, admittedly, a bit of a helicopter mom. I was constantly fussing over her, trying to fix things, trying to make her environment perfectly safe and clean and bereft of obstacles. It took a lot of advice and support from my own mother to finally, gradually learn that by cushioning my daughter against the world around her, she would only learn to be weak. She needs to get those bumps and bruises so that she can toughen up and learn to handle herself in the big, bad world out there. That's difficult for a mom to do: to back off.

Sometimes I still find myself reaching to help her with something I know she can do perfectly well on her own, but I'm getting better. And so is she. My daughter is coping with the darkness and the storm and the uncertainty with quiet resolve. I think she tends to see herself as kind of the leader of the pack here at the daycare, since she's the one who lives here full-time. She's trying to be tough for their sake. The realization of this fact forms a lump in my throat. I'm so proud of her, but I'm also terrified for her. For all of us.

The storm is still raging on, and it's only getting louder and more intense as the minutes tick by. I have no idea how long we have been holed up in this bathroom. My arms are too preoccupied with snuggling these children close for me to reach out and grab my phone to check the time. Besides, what does it matter? We can't go anywhere. We're stuck here, for better or for worse. And then, suddenly...things *do* get worse.

There's a massive crashing sound from outside, almost like an explosion of some kind. All four of the kids gasp in fear and cling to me more desperately, and my own heart races so fast it feels like it might burst out of my chest. The whole house shakes violently, and I worry for a moment that the building might collapse. I wrack my brain, trying to picture what it could have been that caused the noise and vibration. As I sit here, soothing the kids, it hits me: a telephone pole or a tree must have fallen on the house. At the front of the house, it seems like. Which means... the way out must be blocked by something now.

I realize with a jolt how serious this is.

We might actually, truly be stuck here now. Even if I could summon up the reckless courage it would take to go out in the storm and strap four small children into my little sedan and brave the flooded, ravaged roads, it wouldn't matter. We're trapped.

And just when I feel like it can't get any worse, there is another loud sound coming from the same direction. Only this time, it doesn't seem like an accident. There's something oddly intentional about this cracking sound. It happens three more times, even one more forceful than the last. Someone is trying to break in.

For a split second I hope it might be a neighbor

or some cop or relief worker trying to get inside to save us, but that hope is quickly displaced by the more pessimistic prospect that someone is trying to get in to loot our house. That happens when disaster strikes. It's sad and it's ugly to talk about it, but I've seen the news stories. I've read the articles. I know it's a possibility; that someone might see a storm not just as a chaotic disaster, but as an opportunity.

"What is that?" Grant whispers tearfully.

"Is someone here?" asks Weston.

"I don't know, just keep your voices down just in case. I-I'm going to go check it out, okay?" I tell them, gently disengaging myself from the cuddle pile.

"Mommy, no! Don't go!" Dakota insists.

"I'm scared!" Hailey cries, clinging to her whale toy as I slowly let go of them and climb out of the bathtub.

"I know, kiddo, I know. But it's going to be okay. Miss Crystal is not going to let anyone hurt you, alright? You all just stay here and be brave for me. Keep each other safe, alright? I will be back as soon as I can," I assure them. At first, they all move as though to follow me, but Dakota takes charge and opens her pudgy little arms to embrace the other three in a big hug.

"Stay here. My mommy can handle it," she tells them, making my heart soar with love.

"That's right. Mommy's got this," I agree, nodding

as I creep across the darkened bathroom toward the hallway. "I'll be right back."

It's still pitch-black, so I have to reach my arms out and fumble along down the hallway almost blindly, just hoping I don't trip over anything or walk right into danger. If someone is breaking in, then it's up to me to make sure I stop them. Nobody is going to hurt these kids. Not if I have anything to do with it. As I make my way to the front of the house, I can see nothing but darkness through the entryway windows. The wind howls. The house shakes. And there is someone pummeling the front door with a heavy object.

"Go away!" I try to shout, but I'm so afraid that my voice comes out as more of a strangled whisper. I duck down just as the front door lock shatters and the door comes swinging open with a loud bang. I shriek and stumble backward, falling back onto my ass. For a moment, the wind blows a gust of heavy rain through the newly-opened front door, obscuring the figure from view as it steps inside. The intruder is frighteningly tall and broad-shouldered, and I can positively feel the raw strength emanating from him. I reflexively curl up and shield myself with my arms as the intruder slams the door shut and rushes over to me. I flinch, fully expecting him to hit me with a crowbar or whatever it is these people carry around, but instead, there's a large, comforting hand on my shoulder.

"Crystal?" asks the man in a low, deep, almost reverent tone.

The voice is so intimately familiar, but at first I disregard that, since it doesn't make sense. Why would I know this person? I'm trembling and shying away, still half-expecting to be struck.

Again, the man says, "Crystal. It's okay. I'm here."

I know that voice. I've been replaying it in my head for four years now. But it's impossible. He's gone. There's no way it's really him. It can't be.

Still, I can't resist any longer. I slowly lower my arms and peek at him through my fingers, and when I see the startlingly handsome, familiar face in front of me, I gasp in shock. I drop my arms and my eyes go wide. I can't believe it.

"Duncan?" I murmur breathlessly, unable to believe my eyes.

He nods and pulls me into his arms, stroking my hair and rocking me back and forth slightly. I'm so surprised I can't even find the words to say at first.

"You... you're here. I-I don't understand this. Any of this. How are you here right now? Am I dreaming? Am I dead?" I splutter. Duncan chuckles softly, a comforting sound that vibrates down through my whole body.

"It's me. I came for you, Crystal. I'm sorry I didn't get here sooner. This storm— well, I didn't plan for that part," he says.

I shake my head as I pull back to look at him

wide-eyed. "No. Nobody did. This morning, just hours ago, they were calling it a mild tropical storm. And then bam! Out of nowhere it's this huge, scary hurricane. None of us were ready. I wasn't ready. I've just been hiding in my house and the power went out and I know the roads are flooded and—"

"Shh, slow down. It's going to be okay. I'm here now," Duncan says gently, cupping my face in his huge, calloused hands. God, he looks good. Even with his dark hair all flattened down with rain, even through his soaking wet clothes, he looks like a damn Adonis. He's bigger and more muscular than I remember from senior year of high school, back when he was my first love. Back when he was my whole world, when the only future I could see for myself was spending the rest of my life by his side, two parts of a whole. Better together, we always said.

But life has a way of tearing up your best-laid plans. We were supposed to get married or something. Whatever he wanted. Whatever would keep us close. But then his dream of becoming a Navy SEAL diverted our plans. I wanted college, he wanted adventure. We were going to make it work, though, long-distance and everything.

He left, and I applied to colleges. Only to find out weeks later that my plans were on indefinite hold: I was pregnant with Dakota. I was terrified for myself and for Duncan. I loved him more than anything else in the world, and I wanted him to live his dream.

Having a baby at eighteen was already going to derail my plans—I couldn't do that to Duncan, too. So I kept it a secret.

I know how cruel it sounds, but every time I wanted to tell him, he'd send another letter, gushing about his job, about how proud he was to be serving our country. I'd gotten so close, so many times. I wanted him to make his own decisions, but I was afraid, too. I didn't want to be the anchor that kept him stuck here in this small town.

I wanted him to have the adventurous life he craved, and that meant giving him up. It meant living a lie, harboring the truth like a stolen jewel as I became not just a teenage mother, but a single one. It was hard. I made it hard for myself. But I knew that if I truly loved Duncan, it was better to set him free. He was going to make the world a better place, and he couldn't do that if he had a baby to worry about. We kept up communication for a while, and then gradually we drifted apart—mainly because of me. I didn't want him to miss me. I didn't want him to know there was anything *to* miss.

And now he's here. Out of nowhere, looking like the long-lost action hero of my wildest fantasies. He's here to rescue me, even though I don't understand why or how. I realize quickly, though, that this is no time for a drawn-out catch-up session. Maybe some other time. Right now, though, we have to get down to business.

"Duncan, it's not just me here. I-I run a daycare out of my home. I have four terrified little kids hiding in the bathroom. I left them there to come check on the intruder, only...it's not an intruder. It's you," I ramble, nearly forgetting to take a breath.

"Well," he says with a hint of that old humor I loved so much, "I am technically still an intruder. But I'm here to help. Those kids— where are their parents?"

"I don't know," I admit. "Grant, Weston, and Hailey's parents are all at work or something. Cell service is screwed up because of the storm. I can't get a hold of them."

"You said four kids, though. What about the fourth one?" Duncan asks, frowning.

My heart skips a beat. Should I tell him?

No. Of course not. Not right now.

"She's—she's my daughter, actually," I tell him quickly. "Dakota. She's... she's three."

I can see the cogs already turning in his head, even though he looks totally surprised. "You have a daughter?" he asks softly. Tenderly.

Three years old. He doesn't need to know she's almost four. He doesn't need to know that just nine months after our time together, I gave birth. Not right now.

I nod, already feeling the tears burn in my eyes. "Yes. I do. And I don't know how to keep her safe from all that out there. I don't know what to do, Duncan. I'm scared."

"Well, take me to them," he says decisively, offering me a hand to help me up. "Those kids need to be reunited with their parents somehow. I'll help you figure it out."

DUNCAN

I should be speechless. If this weren't in the middle of a literal storm, I would be, in more ways than one. This is all almost too much to take in.

Crystal is far more beautiful than I ever remembered. She's more pristine than a painting, one that someone perfected in the four years since we've seen each other. I feel guilty that I've been thinking about her the way I have, because it doesn't do the real Crystal any justice. Her blonde hair and blue eyes were what drew me in the first time I saw her, and now, I feel like I could get lost in them, if I only gave myself a few seconds to do so.

But I can't. We have so many more pressing matters to tend to.

And her daughter…

I can't let myself think about that, not right now.

The very hint of the thought makes my heart do flips, and that's exactly the kind of emotion that's going to keep me from doing what I consider my duty now. I'm a protector, and I'm going to do my job.

"The roads are partly washed out by now, but there's a Coast Guard blockade on the main road," I say. My instinct is to pace, but I learned long ago not to do that. I maintain confident, calming body language, standing still and moving my hands occasionally as I speak. Crystal listens intently. "You said you've got four kids here total?"

"That's right," she says, and she turns to the hallway and gestures for me to follow. "They're in the bathroom. Kids!" she calls as she guides me along. "Someone's here! He's a...a friend of mine!"

We arrive at the doorway to the bathroom, and I look over the four little ones. I don't see that many kids in my line of work, so seeing them all huddled together here in the middle of a storm guts my heart. Each of them looks up to me with a terrified look on their faces, except for one. One of the girls, a blonde with green eyes, just looks up at me with wonder and curiosity.

"Who are you?" she asks. Her looks are a dead giveaway— this must be Crystal's daughter. There's a kind of brilliance in her eyes that is so familiar and yet so novel that I'm stunned for a moment. I don't know what I should be feeling, and what I *am* feeling is a dizzying rush of sympathy, protectiveness, and love. I have to remind myself yet again not to let myself start thinking too much about this or asking questions. Now isn't the time.

I kneel down slowly so I'm not as intimidating to the four kids, for whatever that's worth.

"I'm Duncan," I say simply. "I'm a friend of Crystal. I'm going to get you all to your parents, is that okay?"

The kids exchange glances with each other, then look to Crystal, who nods softly. I look over my shoulder up at her.

"Do you have a car?"

"Do you not?"

The question takes me by such surprise that I furrow my brow and tilt my head, then remember that most ordinary people do not, in fact, march half the way on foot through a hurricane to get where they're going. I shake my head.

"I landed at the airport just a few minutes before they started diverting flights, and I rented a car to get down here. The storm hit about halfway. I had to... take a few shortcuts on the way, and I happened to get flagged down by Anne."

"Wait, Anne from high school?"

"I know, right? Small towns," I chuckle. "Her husband got trapped on the other side of the bridge, and I wasn't about to just turn around and leave with her or abandon her there. I let her have the car, hiked the rest of the way over here, and decided we could take your car to get the kids somewhere safe."

"Wow," she says, blinking. "That's... a lot."

"I wasn't about to just leave you to ride out the storm on your own," I chuckle.

"How'd you know I was here, though?"

I was hoping she wouldn't ask that. Just like now isn't the time to think about her daughter, it isn't the time to be explaining the big, stupid romantic gesture I tried to put in motion by surprising her with a visit.

"Well, I-"

I'm cut off by the sound of someone knocking loudly at the front door, or what's left of it. My eyes snap down the hall, and I see a man standing there, sticking his head in.

"Hello? Crystal, are you in there? Are you okay?"

My jaw drops. I'd recognize that voice anywhere, and his face hasn't changed much either.

"Jake?" I call, and he freezes. He looks down the darkened hall, but just as he does, one of the lights flickers back on in the hallway, illuminating us. He looks confused for a moment, then his face becomes unreadable for another as he steps inside. Then, his face lights up.

"Duncan?! Is that you?"

I move down the hallway to meet Jake as he steps in, and I grab my best friend from high school in a tight hug as he laughs.

"Duncan! Oh my god, man, of all the times... how are you here right now? Thought you were off being a big shot SEAL?"

"Just thought a hurricane was a good time to drop in and say hello, make sure nobody's drowning just yet," I joke with a wink. "What about you? I thought you'd be out of here by now, the way you were talking at graduation."

"Hah, well, life ain't always what you plan," he chuckles.

Jake Johnson was inseparable from me in high school from day one. We played sports together all four years, and half the summer jobs we took on were gigs we did together. In short, Jake is good people. He was never as ambitious as me, but I'm not going to fault a guy for that. Besides, Jake comes from money. He doesn't need ambition. The guy has a trust fund bigger than some of the bills I've racked up on my missions over the years. That never got in the way of our friendship, though. Seeing him and Crystal here together at the same time feels like a blast from the past in so many ways, all of them making me wish there weren't a hurricane over our heads.

"We'll have to save that story for later," I say.

"No kidding," he says, looking past me to Crystal. "I heard the banging at the front door and wanted to come make sure you were okay. Everything good?"

"Well, besides the fact that I've got the kids here

stranded, I guess so," Crystal says with a smiling yet sarcastic undertone. She turns to me and explains, "Jake lives a couple townhouses down from here."

"Just making sure maniacs like you don't bust in," he says with a chuckle.

"Alright," I say, "this is a hell of a reunion, but it'll have to wait until after we get everyone to safety. Crystal, how many can we fit in your car?"

She winces, which is what I was afraid of.

"It's a two-door sedan," she says. "And I have car seats for the kids. That means I can safely fit three of them in there."

I can see by the look in her eyes that she'll be firm about using the car seats, and frankly, I don't blame her— they're not even her kids, which means that if something happened to them that got them hurt, it would be even more devastating to everyone if it happened because we weren't being safe with the seating arrangements.

"Then I think I see what we need to do here," I say, frowning. "But I don't like it."

"I don't follow," Jake says.

"There are four kids," I say, nodding back to the bathroom.

"Three from the daycare, plus Dakota," Crystal explains. "And we need to get the kids out of here, ASAP. And I'm not letting Dakota away from me for a single second," she adds, looking to me cautiously.

"I'd never ask you to do that," I say, shaking my head. "But we don't have enough room for all of us."

"I'll stay here with Crystal and Dakota," Jake speaks up quickly, looking between both of us. "Dakota knows me, she'll feel safer that way."

"That would be good," I say, nodding to Crystal. "How do you feel about that?"

She looks reluctant, and she bites her lip nervously.

"These are my kids. I really shouldn't be leaving them with someone else, even if it's someone I trust. Maybe I should go, and we make two trips."

"The second the Coast Guard sees you, they're not going to let you go back to the house," I say. I recognize the look in Crystal's eyes. It's her instinct to take all the responsibility on herself as much as possible, including the blame when things go wrong. I have to reassure her that it'll be okay, and I'm hoping the jarring shock of everything going on right now will at least make her more compliant. "I might have some sway with them. I'll go make sure the kids are in safe hands, give the personnel the parents' numbers, and they'll be able to get calls out to them. How does that sound?

She hesitates, but finally, her face softens.

"Works for me," she concedes with a relieved smile. She hurries over to the table and picks up a purse, digging through it and pulling out a set of keys and handing them to me as thunder rolls overhead again. She gives me a cautious look. "Are you sure about this? I don't know how often you work with kids."

"I've got you covered," I say. I look to Jake with a serious nod. "What about you, all good?"

"Definitely," he says with a thumbs-up. I nod.

"I'll be back in less than an hour," I say, and I mean to deliver.

Ten minutes later, the three kids are all in the car, fastened snugly, and Crystal is giving me a terrified wave as I pull out of the driveway. Her car is tidy, almost impeccably so, but there are still hints of her all around—the faint scent of her perfume, a hastily-hidden chewing gum wrapper, and a yoga mat rolled up in the back seat. It's all Crystal, the same girl I left behind four years ago.

"Are you a man or a seal?"

I pause and slowly turn my head to look back at Grant, who's peering at me completely seriously.

"What do you think?" I ask him back as I pull out and start driving northward up the road. The rain is pouring down heavier now, and the windshield wipers can't keep up.

"Can you be both at the same time?" Weston suggests.

"No," Hailey says simply, but the boys seem to take the humble reply seriously.

"I *did* make it here through a lot of water," I say with a smug smile as I carefully drive around a series of branches that are strewn about the road. I see water gushing around the car as I drive it through a few inches of sea and rainwater, and I wonder how much longer this stretch of road will be passable at all.

"What's a seal?" Hailey asks.

"It's like a dog but in water! They're so fat," Weston says. This kid's going places, I can tell.

"A Navy SEAL is a little different from the kind of seal you see at the zoo," I say. It's a silly conversation, but considering how bright the flashes of lightning are against the black sky up ahead, it's better than letting the kids cower in silence in the back.

"How?" Hailey asks.

"We're not as cute," I say with a chuckle.

"Seals are ugly," Hailey says thoughtfully.

Ouch! What does that make me?

Before I can come up with a cute reply, something catches my eye off to the right of the road. There's movement, but something in my gut tells me something's wrong. It's too dark to see much, but lightning flashes long enough for me to see pale faces illuminated around the house. One of the men is holding a baseball bat in front of a shattered window, the other holding the crowbar that pried the plywood off.

Looters? Already?

As I drive by, I see one of them starting to walk toward the car, trying to conceal the baseball bat. I speed up, driving on the opposite side of the road and keeping a clear distance. Just as I'm about to pass him, he breaks into a run and takes a swing at the car. I hear a metallic clank and the sound of breaking glass as he gets one of the tail lights.

I want to spin the car around and see how brave he is when I'm barreling at him at 40mph, but I have children in the car.

I speed up and race down the road as fast as I can without scaring the kids. But as they go quiet, I start to think that damage was already done by the fucker who took a swing at us.

"What was that noise, Mr. Duncan?" Weston asks cautiously after a few moments. I start to think up a cutesy answer, but instead, I decide to turn it into a teaching opportunity.

"That was a man, Weston. Sometimes bad guys like to take advantage of bad situations." I glance over at him with a serious look. "Don't be a bad guy when you get older, okay? People should help each other out. Always."

The kids look thoughtful at that. Well, Hailey doesn't, but she's obviously the youngest, so she was busy looking out the window.

Eventually, we make it to the roadblock. The men out there look like they're fully aware of what a shitty post they're working, but they're determined to stay put. They flag me down before I'm even close enough to slow down. One of them marches up to my window as I roll it down, rain soaking me within seconds.

"Sir, the roads are closed," he barks as he approaches. "What are you-"

"Master Chief Petty Officer Duncan Anderson, US Navy SEAL. I've got three kids from the daycare down the road," I cut him off, flashing my ID with the SEAL notation. The young man raises his eyebrows and opens his mouth to speak before I beat him to it again. "I've got the numbers of these kids' parents, and you've got the vehicles to get them to the mainland. I'm taking care of three more civilians. Are you qualified to get these kids where they need to go, or do I need to ask your CO why you're holding me up?"

CRYSTAL

The second I watch the door close after Duncan rushes out into the rain with the three children, I can feel my heart go flying out after them. Even though my own daughter is still here, safe with me in our home, I'm still petrified for Weston, Grant, and Hailey. They are all such good kids, and I spend so much of my time with them that I almost feel like they are at least partly my own children, too. I love them almost as much as I love Dakota, and the thought of my sweet little angels out there in the cold, pelting rain and the flashes of violent lightning makes me want to curl up on the floor in the fetal position and weep.

It's like three little pieces of my heart have just disappeared through the front door, which now sits crooked in its rectangular frame after Duncan shattered the locks. The guilt I am feeling right now is pulsating higher and higher, nagging at the back of my mind and threatening to drown my entire soul. These kids belong to me. During the work hours, while they are entrusted to my care, they might as well be my own children. I love them. I care for them. I teach them. I laugh with them, cry with them, help them through difficult struggles and celebrate their successes.

When Grant finally overcame his (admittedly irrational) fear that a shark was going to come swimming out of the bathtub drain to chomp his legs off during bath time, it was cause for celebration. I hugged him and kissed his sweet little face, congratulating him on how brave and strong he was. When Weston managed to put together a big 150-piece jigsaw puzzle over the course of a week, I high-fived him and complimented his problem-solving abilities. When Hailey accidentally dropped Whailey in a dirty, oily puddle in the front yard, I held her and rocked her as she cried. The poor little thing was convinced that the gross puddle water had "killed" her best friend. Now, where she got that idea, I have no clue. But kids are often so much smarter and deeper-minded than you'd expect. I put Whailey in the washing machine, then tumbled him dry, and presented him to her good as new. That was another cause for celebration: Whailey had survived a near-death experience.

I have watched these little ones grow, just like all

the kids I look after at my daycare, and they are a vital part of my life. I can't imagine seeing them hurt or lost. The storm has rendered our little town dangerous, with obstacles and closed roads and rough patches all over the place. It hurts my heart to picture them all huddled up in their respective car seats in my little sedan, all of them no doubt crying and whimpering in fear as Duncan drives them… to what? To safety?

The evacuation centers are across town. Their parents are god only knows where. If I don't have cell service, I'm sure Duncan doesn't either. Besides, he doesn't know their parents. Hell, he doesn't even know the kids themselves. And that is why I feel so guilty. Am I a bad caretaker for entrusting these three innocent little souls to a man I have not seen in four years? Sure, he was a stand-up guy back then, but what if something has changed? What if the heroic, good-hearted, gentle Duncan I loved in high school is gone, to be replaced by some big, beefy mystery guy?

Who knows what he's learned, what he's seen, what he's had to go through since joining the Navy SEALs. I am so sure that he's still the same guy, but maybe just tougher and stronger. Maybe even wiser, if he's lucky. But what would their parents say if they knew I've just carted off their children with some near-stranger?

Then again, if there's anyone in the world I

should be able to trust, it would have to be the father of my own child.

I tend to be a very good judge of character, and I have never seen anything but goodness in Duncan's eyes. He's a prince charming. He's a savior of the beaten-down and the broken. Even before he got all that specialized training and experience, he was a good man. Even at the age of eighteen, when most boys are just reckless, selfish bundles of hormonal energy, Duncan was so courteous and high-minded. He wanted to make the world a better place. He treated everyone around him with love and patience.

And then there's Duncan himself. I am terrified for his safety, too. Even though it has been a long, winding four years since he and I were last involved with one another, my heart still beats for him the same way. Every single day. I think of him all the time, so often that it's less like a conscious memory and more like a constant underlying reminder. He never really disappeared from my life, not completely. And not for lack of trying, on my part. I never wanted him to feel tied down by me or by Dakota. All I want is for Duncan to be happy and successful, to live the daring, risk-taking lifestyle he always dreamed of.

So I did my best to push him away, to keep my heart guarded by high fortress walls. I wasn't going to let any other man get inside, but I knew I couldn't hold onto Duncan either. I tried not to think about him. Especially during those early days, when Kota was just an infant. It was easier then, I'll admit, to keep myself distracted. I had a newborn. She cried. She screamed. She nursed. She took up all of my time and all of my heart.

I thought only of her during the days, and thoughts and worries about her consumed many of my nighttime hours, as well. But sometimes, still, when I would lie awake in my bed at night, just listening to Dakota softly breathing through the baby monitor, my mind would wander. And without fail, no matter how many forks in the road and no matter how many obstacles I set to avoid it, my thoughts would mosey on back to Duncan.

I remember in high school when the two of us would meet up under the bleachers by the football field. Not to smoke or drink illegally like most of the kids who huddled there. We just wanted a quiet place away from the prying eyes of our parents, teachers, and other authority figures. A place where we could be alone. Specifically, alone together.

We would hold hands and make out for hours, his hard athlete's body curling around my much smaller, slimmer frame. He could kiss away every dramatic teenage worry that crossed my mind. When I tried out for the cheerleading team and didn't make it, he was there to comfort me. Every year on the anniversary of my father's death, I would hold in all my tears, all my emotions until I could get to those bleachers with Duncan. And then I would let it all out. He would hold me, promise me everything would be alright. He has always possessed an almost supernatural ability to calm me down and make the world seem a little bit brighter, more hopeful.

No wonder I've missed him so much.

And no wonder I feel so damn guilty for hiding the truth about Dakota from him. Sometimes, over the years, I would be overcome with the guilt. I would tearfully open up my social media accounts and search for Duncan's name. There was never very much there— he rarely updated his feed. I would write out a long-winded message to send him, an explanation of why I've hidden Dakota's existence from him, why I've never told him he's a father. But at the last second, I always deleted the message. I let the moment pass.

But now that he's here in town, how can I keep it a secret from him any longer?

Doesn't he deserve to know?

Would he hate me for hiding the truth from him?

If the positions were reversed... if someone had hidden my child from me for almost four years...

But what if I was right in the first place, that his life is better without Dakota and me to bog it down. He's having the adventures he always wanted. He's protecting our country! I could tell that much just by looking at him, by reading the history and memory in those gorgeous green eyes so similar to Kota's eyes. How could I rain on his parade?

I'm interrupted from my thoughts by a haughty, almost indignant male voice from behind my left shoulder. "What are you doing?"

I gasp in surprise and swivel around to face Jake, who's regarding me with a sort of an amused expression, his arms crossed over his chest. He tilts his head to one side and looks me up and down, grinning. "You look like you've just seen a ghost," he chuckles.

I quickly force a smile and tuck my hair behind my ears— a nervous habit I've had since high school. "Sorry. I'm just anxious about Duncan and the kids," I admit.

Jake clucks his tongue with sympathy, only it doesn't feel wholly genuine. "Ah, don't worry about them. They'll be fine. Besides, you're safe here with me," Jake says, waving his hand dismissively.

"I just hope they get to safety, that's all. I keep imagining something horrible happening," I sigh, shaking my head. "Thank you for coming over, by the way. You didn't have to."

Jake looks positively glowy at my appreciation. He takes a step closer, which makes me feel oddly uncomfortable. I have no logical reason to fear him. After all, he has been my next-door neighbor for close to a year now, and we were friends back in high school. In fact, he was Duncan's best friend.

The two of them played team sports together all the time. When I dated Duncan, Jake often tagged along. I don't think it was ever much of a third wheel situation, though. I always did my best to include him so it wasn't awkward.

"Of course, I came over. I wouldn't just leave you here stranded alone. That's more Duncan's bag, huh?" he jokes rather harshly. I stiffen up, frowning.

"Well, he did show up out of nowhere to help me," I point out.

A flicker of something dark crosses Jake's face, and my heart skips a beat. I have never seen him as a combative or even assertive person. He's just an old friend who has drifted apart from me a little over the years. Just a neighbor who waves at me when we check our mail or returns my packages when they get sent to the wrong address. But there's something in Jake's eyes right now that chills me to the very bone.

"Well, I mean, he *did* leave you four years ago," Jake says coldly.

I blink in surprise at the stark statement. "He didn't leave me. He just... left. It was an amicable breakup. It was mutual," I explain softly. Dakota pokes her head out from around the corner, looking at me with wide green eyes. I can tell she's confused, trying to put two and two together. She doesn't know Duncan. She barely knows Jake. But even she can sense that this conversation is heading down a shadowy path.

I don't want her to hear any of this, so I give her a smile and say, "Hey sweetie, can you go back to the bathroom where it's safe? Mr. Johnson and I are going to have a grown-up conversation in the kitchen, okay?"

Kota nods balefully. "Okay, Mommy," she answers in a small voice. I ruffle her hair as she passes by, toddling down the hall to the bathroom. As soon as the door is shut, I turn back to Jake and jerk my head toward the kitchen so he can follow. He smiles almost deviously. Like this is what he's been hoping for all along.

To get me alone.

As soon as we step into the kitchen, Jake corners me, slowly walking me back against the kitchen counter. I notice for the first time that he's much taller and broader than I am. He's not as thick and muscular as Duncan, but he's definitely got a leg up over me. I swallow hard, hoping that the warning sirens blaring in the back of my mind are just misguided. But when he starts talking in a low, growly voice, I know something is very wrong.

"You know, I have been watching you over the past several months," he says, smiling.

A pit starts to form in my stomach. "Oh? Uh, have you?" I ask, startled.

He nods slowly. "Yes. I wanted to keep an eye on you and… the little one."

"Wow. Well, that is very kind of you, but it's not necessary. I've got everything under control here. I don't need someone to watch over me," I explain as politely as I can.

Jake doesn't falter for a second, walking me back so that I'm pinned against the counter. I can feel his body heat radiating off of him. I can smell his slightly musty breath. His eyes bore into mine deeply, like he's trying to read my mind or something.

"No, you do need me. You've always needed me, even though you've never realized it yourself. Ever since high school, you've been ignoring me. Pretending I don't exist. I moved here so I could be closer to you, Crystal. I thought that once we were next door to each other you couldn't ignore me anymore. But you... you're so oblivious," Jake growls.

"Jake, please stop. You're freaking me out," I murmur.

"Oh, am I?" he says, raising an eyebrow but not backing off an inch. "Well, then, that's an improvement. At least you're noticing me now. Is that all it takes? To get Duncan out of the way first?"

"What the hell are you talking about?" I ask, glaring at him.

He glares right back and goads me, "Come on, Crystal. Like you don't know. Don't play stupid with me. You and I both know that this has been simmering for a long, long time. Duncan left you. Abandoned you *and* Dakota. He left to go play hero in some foreign land. But me? I stuck around. I stayed close. I turned down jobs in other cities just to stay here with you. I knew that if I left, there would be no one around to keep tabs on you. And with that sweet little girl you've got here—"

"Don't you talk about my daughter," I interrupt tersely between gritted teeth.

Jake looks mildly taken aback, like he never expected to get a rise out of me. Then the surprise fades to smug satisfaction. "Ooh. There's a little glimpse of the spitfire I knew you were all along. Underneath that sugar-sweet, prudish facade, you're a little spicy, aren't you? There's a tiger lurking inside this little pussycat, and I'm going to be the one to wake it up."

"Yeah, right," I scoff. "You may have watched me all this time like a damn stalker, but you don't know me, Jake. You never knew me. And you never, ever will."

"Shut up!" he snarls, suddenly grabbing me by the arms and hoisting me up onto the counter. I yelp and try to wriggle out of his grasp, but he quickly pins me there, leaning in close to whisper in my ear. "I've done my time. I've been so, so patient with you, Crystal. Waiting for you to notice me, to realize who you truly belong to. Duncan's gone. I'm here. Him showing up to try to play hero again changes nothing, and I'm getting really damn tired of waiting for you to wake up. So I'm going to have to wake you up by force. I didn't want it to be this way, but you've given me no other choice."

The storm rages on overhead, the winds howling like a distant banshee while Jake dives forward to kiss me. I yank my head to one side so that he misses, his lips landing on my cheek instead. But this refusal only seems to stoke his fire. He grabs my thighs and squeezes them as his teeth graze the ticklish skin of my neck. I try to jerk away, but he hooks his fingers through my belt loops and holds me still, attempting to pull down my shorts with one hand while his other hand snakes up underneath my purple t-shirt.

"No!" I gasp, torn between wanting to yell for help and not wanting my innocent daughter to get caught up in this. I bite my lip to keep from screaming as I do my best to knee him in the chest. But he's too fast, too tough for me. Jake is too big, and he overpowers me easily. Tears spring to my eyes as he begins to touch my skin, his hand slipping up under my shorts. There is nobody coming to save me. My hero already showed up and left.

Then, I just happen to glance over and see a peanut-butter-encrusted blade of a knife lying on the stack of dishes in the sink. Without a second thought, my hand darts out and grabs it. Just as Jake is rearing back to unzip his jeans, I brandish the knife out in front of me, my arm shaking as I stare him down with pure terror.

He stops short and holds his hands up, glaring first at the knife, then up at me. He grits his teeth, almost sneering at me in his anger.

"You bitch," he snarls.

"Don't you touch me ever again," I mumble, fighting back tears so I can look tougher and more resilient than I feel. There's a long pause while he sizes me up, trying to decide whether or not I'm worth the trouble. Then, finally, he rolls his eyes and takes a step back.

"Fine. Not today. I get it. The storm's got you all worked up. You wouldn't be any fun for me right now, anyway. That's okay. I've waited this long, I can wait a little longer," Jake says, with an almost chilling degree of casualness. He smooths down his shirt and zips his jeans back up, shrugging. A shark-like grin spreads across his face.

"Another time, then, hmm?" he murmurs. "Don't worry. I'll make it special."

And with that, he stalks out of the kitchen, leaving me sitting on the counter in total shock, still gripping the knife. My whole body is paralyzed with fear. Slowly, with my hand trembling violently, I set the knife back down in the sink. I swipe my hands over my eyes to dry my tears and take a long, slow deep breath. I hear the door open and shut, and I let out a sigh of relief.

I can't let Dakota see me like this. She's so intuitive, she'll know immediately something is wrong, and I just need to catch my breath and come to terms with what happened. It's another several minutes before I can even force myself to move, I'm so overwhelmed with shock.

I can't believe it. The guy I've known since high school, Duncan's own best friend. My neighbor. The sweet, popular, quiet guy who tagged along on a lot of our teenage adventures. I never saw it coming. I never expected him to turn out to be a viper in disguise.

He's been watching me. A chill runs down my spine. All this time, I've thought I was safe. I assumed everything was normal. But all along, there has been a secret sleeper agent living right next door, just waiting for the right occasion to trap me. I wrack my brain, wondering why the hell he's never tried anything until now. I've been home alone so many nights, just Dakota and me. I make sure to keep the window blinds shut. I keep my doors locked constantly.

A jolt shakes my whole body. Maybe that's it: he just needed an easy way in. Offering to stay with me while Duncan left was just his way of circumventing the locks. There is a predator in my home, and *I* let him in.

Finally, I manage to slide down off the counter, although my legs still feel as wobbly as jello, and I start to make my way toward the hallway to go join Kota and make sure she's not too freaked out by the storm. But when I look down the hall toward the bathroom, my heart stops.

The door is open. I can see right into the bathroom, and my daughter isn't there.

"No," I mumble, swiveling around to limp numbly back toward the front of the house. "No, no, no." I feel like I'm inside a nightmare, like I'm wading through molasses. I can't go any faster, and the world around me is melting away. My heart is pounding so fast that it's hard to breathe. Every neuron in my brain is screaming with panic and dread. As I'm coming around the corner to the entryway, my whole world starts to fall apart.

The front door is closed. I heard it open and shut, right after... right after Jake...

"Dakota?" I call out, my voice trembling.

There's no reply.

I wait a moment, frozen with fear and confusion, my mind not working. The house is silent. The storm howls and crashes outside. I don't even have to check the rooms to know my daughter isn't in them. She's not in the house. She is... somewhere else.

"Dakota!" I cry, throwing open the door just to be confronted with rain pelting my face and body, the water rushing up my front steps to splash into my home. Shielding my eyes from the rain, I look around in complete horror. There's no one in sight. Not Jake. Not Dakota. Not a single soul. The flood waters have completely surrounded my townhouse, and they're rising even higher by the second.

"He took her," I gasp breathlessly, feeling faint as my breaths rip raggedly and painfully through my body. I press a hand over my heart, struggling to stay upright as the world around me comes crashing down. "He took my baby!" I scream, crumpling to the filthy, wet ground.

DUNCAN

"This is easily the worst storm any of us have ever seen," says the seaman as I watch them load up the last of the three kids in a secure jeep to take them back to the mainland. "The news is going to be all over this fiasco before the storm is even over."

Almost as soon as I flashed my ID, the whole group sprang into action. I may not technically have authority over these guys, but my reputation seems to precede me. Weston raises a hand to wave goodbye to me, and I wave back at him before the door gets closed and a couple of the Coast Guardsmen start driving them to the mainland and to safety. They'll be far safer with them in that military vehicle than with me in anything I'm going to be driving in the near future, I imagine. They got in touch with their parents, who it turns out

103

have been hovering at the other Coast Guard blockade at the bridge, trying to get in and find their kids.

"And why wasn't the news all over it in time for these people to get to safety?" I ask, crossing my arms.

"Took everyone by surprise," he replies, shaking his head. "This thing was supposed to be small. It just picked up speed and strength out of nowhere. Now it's the fucking apocalypse, and it caught us all with our pants down."

"What's the situation on the mainland?"

"Bad," he says simply. "Flooding and fires everywhere. Traffic pile ups. Imagine what's going on here but with about ten times as many people. We're doing everything we can, and that's the most I can say."

"Keep it up," I say, giving him an encouraging nod. "We need as many men and women like you all out here on the ground."

"You're really heading back into that nightmare, aren't you?" he asks, looking at me uncertainly. "Look, I won't stop you, but officially speaking, I can't let you leave here."

"Then I slipped away when you weren't looking," I suggest, already heading back to Crystal's car. I turn my back on him and get back into the little vehicle, turning the engine on and watching the Guardsman shake his head in disbelief as I pull out and turn around, driving headfirst into the inky blackness ahead of me.

Lightning seems to boom every few minutes, sometimes in such quick succession that I'd think a bombing raid was going on, if I didn't know better.

I don't see the looters in the same spot as before when I drive by. I'm almost disappointed. Being able to teach those bastards who scared the kids a lesson wound be some much needed stress relief right about now.

The drive back to the townhouse is a lot less harrowing, thanks to the simple fact that three small lives aren't depending on me anymore. I still have to wind through a few yards and in paved roads along the way, because the waters are getting higher, and Crystal's car is even less suited to fording little rivers of flood water than my rental SUV was. Getting Crystal, Kota, and Jake out of here is going to be an issue, but I'm already formulating a route, watching out for places that look like they'll be less flooded than others in a few more minutes, maybe an hour.

The best case scenario is that I convince the three of them to stay put and bunker down until we see a break of some kind, even if it's just the slightest reprieve in the storm. I hate being apart from Crystal and her daughter, but I'm glad Jake showed up when he did. It makes me feel a bit less like I abandoned them, and helps keep my nerves steady.

Jake was always sturdy in a crisis. I tried to talk

him into joining up with me a few times, but he always had different plans. I guess that's why we never kept in touch. In high school, we got along fine, but after graduation, we were just too different to find much common ground.

I can feel the wind threatening to blow the car around if I lose control of it for just a second, and that isn't helped by the fact that the rain is so intense that hesitating for any moment could leave the car submerged in too much water.

As if on cue at that thought, I pull up to the townhouse to find the floodwaters rising too high to cross in this little car. I curse and pull up to the highest ground I can find, then get out and lock the car up. I can't promise it will be safe, but it's better than guaranteeing that it will get flooded if I try to get it closer to the townhouse.

I wade into the water and slosh across to the door, hurrying up to it and shaking some of the water off me. Not that it makes much of a difference, with the rain pouring down.

But as soon as I put my hand on the door, I feel it. Something is wrong.

I burst into the house and look around, and when the sound of sobbing reaches my ears, my whole body goes on high alert. It's Crystal. I turn and see her huddled against the wall on the floor not far from the entrance, curled up into a ball and shaking.

"Crystal!" I say in a low, comforting tone as I

stoop down to scoop her into my arms. She falls into them naturally, as if on reflex. I slide my strong hands around her and hug her close to me as her whole body shudders, and my eyes widen as I feel her trembling. "Crystal, what's wrong? What happened? Where's Jake?"

"She's gone!" Crystal's words are mumbled and half-stifled by choking sobs, but I can make those two words out through the mess. I look down at her and try to get her to look up at me, but she's inconsolable.

My heart leaps to my throat. "Crystal, I need you to take deep, slow breaths. I'm here. Breathe. It's going to be okay. What happened?"

"He took her!" she manages. Her face is swollen and red, and tears are streaming down her face. Finally, she looks up at me through eyes I can barely see through the tears and her puffy eyelids, and the sight of her breaks my heart. Crystal has always been so full of light and life that seeing her like this makes me feel some of the pain she's experiencing. It's agonizing, and even more so not knowing what to do about it. "Jake took Kota!"

The words hit me like lightning.

"What do you mean, took her? What happened, Crystal?"

But she just stammers the same thing over and over again, clearly in shock. I pick her up carefully and carry her to the couch, where I set her down and kneel in front of her. I'm so tall that I'm still on eye-level with her. She's still trembling and sobbing, but the movement seems to have done something to snap her out of her heartbroken haze, and she starts trying to get a hold of herself. I have training for crisis situations, but not much of it covers how to console someone who's in the middle of a panic attack. I have to rely on instinct.

So I take her hands in mine and squeeze them softly, letting my thumb stroke over the tops of her hands as I speak as comfortingly as I can.

"The other kids are safe. The Coast Guard is taking care of them. Your car made it through with no problems. I'm here. That's it, slow, deep breaths. Focus on my eyes, something you can center yourself on. Anything. There we go. Can you tell me what happened?"

She finally manages to bring her ragged breathing to a slower pace, getting control of it and looking at me with wide eyes before she sniffs once more. The panic is just under the surface of a loose lid, but she's so strong that she can hold it in long enough to speak.

"When you left, Jake, he... he got... different. He changed."

"Changed how?"

"He got aggressive," she says, and her voice cracks as she does. She puts her hands over her face and loses it for a few moments. I stroke her arms and rub her shoulders, shushing her softly to try to relax her. It seems to work, and soon, she has her bearings again. "He wanted me to... he made a pass at me as soon as you were gone."

My eyes widen, and I feel utter shock working its way through my body. Jake? The Jake I know, the one who was my best friend growing up? That... that can't be right, can it? I brush the hair out of Crystal's face and stroke it before taking her hands again and nodding softly.

"Take your time. Slow breaths."

"I don't know what I did to bring it on," she says, shuddering. "I always thought he was just a friend, but he... he started talking like he *wanted* me. I-I think he has for a long time."

The pit in my stomach is growing with every passing second. I can barely believe what I'm hearing, but this is Crystal— I'd believe anything she says.

I've suspected for a long time that Jake has at the very least noticed Crystal. We were teenagers back then, teenagers *notice* just about everyone at that age. But now?

"What did he say?"

"He said he'd been watching me," she says with a shiver, her face cringing in embarrassment and disgust. "He... he wanted me to feel the same way about him. But I-I didn't, I don't, I mean-"

"I understand," I say, nodding, but my brow is furrowed. "You two never had anything?"

"No! I've been alone since… I mean, you were…" she struggles with the words, shaking her head with wide eyes. "I never thought… oh God," she groans, sobbing again for a moment. My heart is shattering along with hers. I never in a million years would have thought that Jake would be anything but a perfect gentleman, but seeing Crystal here in ruins because of something that happened… I'm starting to see it unfolding in my head all to clearly.

"Did he hurt you?" I ask urgently, and I start checking her hands and arms over for signs of a struggle, already dreading the worse.

"I tried to tell him no, but he got angry," she says, voice cracking again. "I had no idea what to do, I… I was so scared. I've never seen him like this. I got hints of it every now and then, but I thought… I thought he was harmless!"

"This isn't your fault, Crystal," I say. "Tell me what happened."

"He… he touched me."

I already didn't have any doubts about what Crystal is saying, as horrific as it is, but those three words stir something deep within me: rage. Fury swells up in me like a storm, anger and indignation all at once. My mouth falls open as anger boils just under the surface.

"What?!"

Crystal nods, trying hard to keep herself from falling apart again.

"He tried to force himself on me, and I... I didn't know what to do, I just grabbed the knife and waved it at him, and he backed off. He left me alone for a minute, and I heard the door close, and I didn't want Kota to see me all messed up, and I was so shocked I couldn't move, and- and- and-"

"And he took Kota?" I finish for her with wide, horrified eyes. Crystal's face goes red again, and she nods before sobbing into my shoulder.

I wrap my arms around her as everything clicks in my head, and I realize I have the full story, as much as it horrifies me. Jake has desired Crystal in a much worse way than I ever imagined. Just like those looters who swung a bat at us, the storm brings evil out in weak people, so Jake tried to take advantage of Crystal's vulnerable situation. When she fought back, he snapped and struck back at her in her most vulnerable point imaginable.

The memories I have of Jake, the man I thought I knew, it all melts away in that instant, faster than a wisp of smoke dissipating.

Jake is not the man I knew.

He hurt Crystal. He might hurt Dakota, a mere child.

He isn't my friend. He's a monster.

"How long ago?" I ask suddenly, my training

kicking into gear. I look at her squarely, and she thinks for a moment before sniffing.

"I-I don't know, I haven't been able to keep track of time. Not long? Oh God, the storm! We have to go get her!"

She tries to stand up and race to the door right then and there, but I hold her back.

"Wait," I urge her, even as she struggles against me. "Crystal, the storm is too strong, I can't let you just rush out there! Do you know where he went?"

"His house is just down from here, but water was flooding everything, he- he could be anywhere!"

"He can't have gone far," I say, making my way to the window. "He's probably at his house. If we hurry, we can-"

I trail off as a familiar noise reaches my ears, and my heart starts to sink.

"What?" Crystal asks anxiously, taking a step toward me and following my gaze to the ceiling.

Up overhead, I can hear a horrible sound coming from the skies. It sounds like a distant howling growing stronger and louder by the second. Soon, it melts into the sound of a train approaching, roaring over us and swallowing the whole house.

"It's a tornado!"

CRYSTAL

*E*very nerve in my body is pinging, sending emergency signals back to my brain, begging to know what the hell I am supposed to do now. It's like my whole heart is swollen with pain, aching with dull agony with every beat. It's hard to breathe. My throat feels thick and dry, like I must have somehow swallowed a handful of cotton balls.

The thoughts ricocheting through my head like little marbles in a pinball game are not coherent. They aren't helpful. It's just a cacophony of warning bells, ringing so loudly and so persistently that the rumbling din of the hurricane can't even compete. Distantly, somewhere in the fog, I can make out Duncan's voice. Deep, growling, deliberate. Begging me to snap out of it. Trying desperately to reach for me in the fog, but unable to grasp hold of me completely.

I feel like I'm not even made of flesh and bone anymore. I am a wisp, reduced to nothingness by shock and terror. I don't feel like a regular person. Maybe that's why Duncan can't reach me and pull me back out of the ominous mist settling in around my panicked thoughts. Not anymore. Not now that a significant piece of my heart has been swept away into the rushing waters of the flood, no doubt dragged along by an evil man with evil intentions. My baby girl. My angel. My tiny best friend. My bright white light in the darkest hour. My little flame.

"Gone. Just like that," I can hear my lips murmuring, even though I still can't feel a damn thing beyond the numbness and the dull pain. "I am a bad mother. I always thought I was doing a pretty damn good job of handling all this on my own."

Duncan's huge hands land on my shoulders, gripping them softly as he gives me a gentle shake. "You are not a bad mother. You're a brilliant caretaker," he assures me in a low growl. But I am wholly unconvinced.

I go on, "In fact, I was so confident in my own abilities as a caretaker that I made a living out of it. I opened a damn daycare in my home, Duncan. I told other parents that I could totally handle it. There was enough of my energy and strength to go around. But I guess I was wrong. All along, I was a bad mother. An unfit guardian. This is all my fault and now it's my baby girl who's going to pay for it."

"No, Crystal. That's not going to happen. Your daughter is going to be just fine. We're going to find her and bring her home and everything will be alright. I promise you that," he insists, reaching up to cup my cheek. I lean into his warm touch as a tear rolls down my cheek to streak over his fingers. I shake my head slightly.

"It's impossible. He—he took her, Duncan. Right out of my home. Right out from under my nose. How could I have been so stupid? How could I have been so selfish? I should have ran to her, right after he… he…" I sob, my shoulders shaking as my legs go weak beneath me. I feel like I could crumple to the ground at any second now. I know Duncan will hold me up, even though the last thing I deserve right now is his kindness. I'm a wretched failure of a human being, and no amount of tenderness will convince me otherwise.

"Crystal, you are many things, but you are not and have never been selfish. And you're not stupid, either. I remember the kind of grades you made in high school. You made the rest of us look like dunces," Duncan jokes gently, gazing hard into my eyes. I can tell he's trying to lighten my mood and distract me from the pain streaking through my body like a thousand tiny knives, but there's no way. It breaks my heart just that little pinch more to realize just how identical the green of his gaze is to Dakota's. She has her father's eyes. God, I miss them. What if I never get the chance to look into my daughter's eyes again?

What if Duncan never gets that chance, either? I have kept her hidden from him all these years, self-ishly guarding her from him. And for what? To give him a better chance at the life he dreamed of? To keep her all to myself? I feel like a fool for ever thinking I could manage all of this by myself. Clearly, I cannot, because this never would have happened if I was a good parent. I'm not good enough.

And now that asshole is going to do god only knows what with my angel.

Suddenly, a burst of energy pierces through the darkness shrouding around me and propels me away, out of Duncan's soothing grasp, out of the house. I can't be in here anymore, listening to the clock tick on the wall and the rain patter on the roof. I can't be here surrounded by Dakota's toys, her tiny clothes, the framed photographs of her as a baby smiling toothlessly for the camera. I can't stand here, drowning in memories and heartache.

With a violent thrust, I shove myself back away from Duncan and dart to the front door. I fling it open and go bolting out into the heavy rain, falling so hard that it's nearly sideways in the gusty wind. I look around frantically, as though somehow Jake and Kota will appear through the dense rain and the darkness. The yard is flooding all the way up to my knees now. I shiver as the rain soaks through my clothes, causing goosebumps to pop up on my skin. Dizzy, disoriented, but utterly determined, I turn toward Jake's house.

It's on a bigger lot than mine, with a large yard and driveway. His car, the silver four-door that's usually parked in the drive, is missing. That must be how he got away with her so fast. And yet, I still feel compelled to run to his house, shatter my fist through a window, and search the house for them just in case. What if the car is gone so that I'm deceived into thinking they're not home? Just like the door opening and shutting so quickly after I fought him off! Maybe it's all on purpose to confuse me! My thoughts are maddeningly incoherent, and my body is so numb that when I try to start wading across my yard toward Jake's, I can hardly force my legs to lift up and down. But I have to. I have to get there. I have to find my baby…

Just as I'm about to stumble and fall face-forward into the water with a great splash, I feel two powerful hands grip my arms and yank me back-ward. I'm pulled back against a hard, muscular chest, and the two arms wrap around my body, dragging me through the flood waters. I realize with a jolt that it's Duncan trying to bring me back to my house. He doesn't want me to go looking for Kota.

He won't let me. I start trying to fight back, kicking and writhing in his arms, screaming out for my daughter even though the heavy rain and howling wind are loud enough to fully drown out any human cry.

"No! Let me go! I have to save her! Please, let me find my baby!" I scream, but Duncan is stronger than me. Much stronger. He all but carries me back into the house, kicking and screaming. I'm trembling all over, whether from the panic or the cold rain I can't really tell.

Duncan pulls me into the house and slams the door closed. As soon as he loosens his grip on me for a second, I crumple to the floor, drawing my knees up to my chest and burying my face in my arms while I shiver and sob. Duncan kneels down next to me and wraps his arms around me, kissing the top of my soaking wet head and stroking my dripping hair.

"We will find her, Crystal. But not like this. Not now. The tornado is too close. We have to keep safe so we can save her," he murmurs, close to my ear.

But my mind is miles away by now, churning through memories. "I lost her once before," I mumble, still not looking up. "I found out for the first time what it feels like to be missing a part of your very soul. It was… it was years ago. She was barely two years old, just getting the hang of running around without me to help her. She never wanted my help anyway. She was— she is so stubborn. So independent," I whisper, taking a big breath. I go on.

"We went to this big shopping mall out of town. Two floors with an escalator and everything. We went up together, hand-in-hand. She was determined to walk. Didn't want to be carried. Dakota wanted to be a big girl. Who was I to tell her no? We got to the top floor and it was so crowded. People everywhere. There was one of those stupid mall pageants going on. Little girls dressed up in frilly dresses and red lipstick everywhere. Dakota... she was distracted. And confused. This aggressive pageant mom with huge blonde hair bumped into us, causing her own little daughter to fall down and start crying. Even though it was her own fault, that lady started picking a fight with me. She was shoving me around, shouting about how I need to watch myself. In the chaos, Dakota disappeared. I managed to get away from that pageant lady and I was so terrified, screaming out for my daughter. I was only twenty. Everyone thought I was just some teen causing trouble. They kept shushing me. I was interrupting the pageant ceremony. But I didn't care. I was terrified. My baby was missing. I had never known fear like that before," I admit, tears streaming down my face.

"What happened?" Duncan asks gently.

I finally look up at him, my lip trembling. "I found her. Turns out, she got scared of the crowd and went wandering away. Ended up on the down escalator. Can you imagine? Just a tiny two-year-old alone on the escalator in a crowded mall? Well, I took off after her. I caught up and carried her out of that mall and we've never been back there since. I thought that was the worst fear I'd ever experience. I thought that was the peak. But I was wrong. God, I was so wrong."

I collapse into sobs again just as there's an even louder whirring sound overhead. The whole house is violently shaking, dishes crashing out of cabinets in my kitchen, pictures falling off the shelves in my living room. Duncan gets a grim, resigned look on his face and scoops me up into his arms.

We reach the bathroom and he closes the door, the lights all flickering and flashing with frantic energy. He lays out a couple towels on the floor and then pulls me down with him so that we're lying side by side. As the tornado whirls louder and louder, Duncan tugs me close and embraces me, kissing my cheek, my neck, my shoulders while his hands stroke my wet hair.

"Come on, let's take off these wet clothes. You're shivering," he whispers. I dutifully let him strip off my shirt, shorts, bra, and panties. I kick off my soaked tennis shoes and socks, lying there utterly naked. There's a small part of my brain that knows I should probably feel self-conscious, naked in front of this glorious man I haven't seen in four years. But then again, he's the only man who has ever seen me this way. He's the only one I've ever slept with.

To comfort me, Duncan caresses me all over, his hands running over my stomach, my filled-out hips and ass, my thick thighs. He touches me with the exact same reverence and admiration he did four years ago. The tornado sounds louder and louder, almost deafening. I tremble, so overwhelmed with sorrow and fear. But Duncan is determined to distract me, to ease me through the pain. I feel his hands slide over my breasts, not groping crudely the way Jake did, but sensually. I know it's for my pleasure more than his own. And when he slides a hand down between my shivering thighs, I don't stop him. I need whatever it is he's offering. I need it like a plant needs sunlight.

So I open, unfolding and blooming for him like a rose. I wiggle closer to him, feeling his hard cock straining against my ass through the damp fabric of his jeans. I rub up against him, egging him on, reveling in the sensation of his hard length pressing into me. His hand slips down between my legs, cupping my mound first with his large, warm hand. I can feel myself getting wetter by the second, already exhilarated with fear and panic, which is such close kin to arousal. The adrenaline pumping through my veins makes every stroke of his fingers around my clit feel amplified by a million degrees. Every touch makes me shudder and sigh. Duncan kisses the back of my neck while he manipulates my clit, then slowly slides two fingers inside of me, hooking them at the ends to expertly stroke my g-spot deep within.

"Oh my God," I moan, arching back against him. My thighs tremble and my body stiffens up as he slides his digits in and out of my slick pussy, pleasuring me and distracting me while the tornado spins overhead, screaming louder than a freight train. My moans and whimpers are almost swallowed up completely by the stormy din, but Duncan can feel it when I come, my pussy pulsing and clenching around his fingers. A rush of powerful endorphins surges through my body and I feel, for a few moments, sweet relief.

There's the distraction I need to get through this dark hour.

And I want more.

Luckily, Duncan is on the exact same page. He moves out from behind me, pushing me to lie flat on my back as he scoots down to kneel between my legs. He pushes my thighs wide open and dips down to breathe in my fragrant sex. I prop myself up on my elbows to watch wide-eyed as he bends to lap up my sweet juices, devouring my clit and over-sensitive folds with his sensual lips. His tongue flicks over my clit as he licks up and down, making me shiver and go weak. My elbow gives out and I fall back, arching and thrusting my hips involuntarily, bucking against his face as he eats me out. He moans with appreciation, tasting me deeply, sending delicious vibrations up through my body.

The lights flicker dramatically as he devours me, bringing me closer and closer to the edge while the hurricane hurls tornadoes in our direction. The house is shaking down to its very foundation, and I know distantly that there's a great chance of danger here. Even death.

But the pleasure keeps me afloat, keeps me distracted from my anxiety and panic and fear. It keeps me riveted in this sweet spot, this lull between fantasy and reality where I can just give in and let my body take whatever release and relief it craves. I suspend my thoughts, pushing all that dread and panic and guilt into a dark, shadowy corner where it can no longer wound me. At least for now. At least until the storm passes. I can't do anything to save my baby right now— I need to survive this so I can fight for her. And this, the pleasure and the distraction, is just what I need to get through to the other side.

The lights go bright for a full ten seconds, almost blindingly bright, just as Duncan's tongue tips me over the edge. I come again and again, twitching and writhing on the bathroom floor with the man of my dreams kneeling between my thighs. He tastes me like I'm something forbidden, like he's been dreaming of this for ages.

"You taste just like heaven," he groans, looking up at me and licking his lips. I'm too overwhelmed with bliss to even form a response, but he dives back in, lapping me up and massaging my clit with his rigid tongue. Finally, it gets to be almost too much, and I need a break. I gently nudge his head away from my cunny and sit up. He looks at me almost quizzically as I crawl over to him on my knees. I reach down and tug at the waistband of his jeans, peering into his eyes deeply, pleadingly.

Without a single word, he understands. Duncan nods and strips off his shirt, then his jeans, boxers, socks, and boots. His massive, hard cock springs free, making my heart skip a beat. He's even bigger than I remember, and my mouth waters at the sight of it. He stands up to lean back against the bathroom counter while I kneel in front of him, almost in a worshipful position. The lights flicker around us as I lean in and pull his full, rigid length into my mouth with a satisfied moan.

Duncan groans and rocks his hips gently, fucking my mouth so that the tip of his cock brushes against the back of my throat. I wrap one hand around the base of his shaft, pumping up and down in tandem with my mouth, while the other hand fondles his sac. I love the sensation of his thickness stretching my cheeks, filling up my mouth with his silky, powerful shaft. I bob up and down, moaning and whimpering while his hand presses softly at the back of my head. He thrusts gently, almost making me gag, but I swallow down every drop of his salty, glorious pre-cum.

I reach down to feel my pussy getting even wetter, turned on by the way his cock feels in my mouth. I suck harder, bobbing up and down faster and faster while my hand works the base of his rod. I can feel him tensing up, getting closer and closer as the tornadoes wail outside. We could die together here. It's possible. But right now, all either of us can feel is the immense pleasure and exhilaration of being together again, of our bodies uniting.

Finally, just before I can bring him to climax, Duncan pushes me back with a soft nudge. His cock slips out of my mouth with a wet pop and I look up at him with a plaintive, pleading expression, licking my lips. He crouches down on the towels with me, sitting down. I crawl over to him, leaning in to kiss him passionately. I can taste myself on his lips and I know he can taste himself, too, as our tongues probe into each other's mouths. His hands caress my breasts, my back, my ass. He grasps my hips and moves me closer, guiding me to straddle him so that the head of his engorged shaft is pressing at my slick opening. With one little wiggle I could slide him inside of me. My whole body tenses with anticipation.

I know what I want. And I think he just might give it to me.

Duncan looks me square in the eyes, searching

for the answer to a question he has not asked me yet. I bite my lip, waiting.

He opens his mouth to speak, and though the tornado is too loud for me to hear a word of what he says, I can read his lips perfectly. "Do you want this?"

I nod and mouth the words, "Yes. Please."

A mere second later, the lights go out again, plunging us into darkness. But that doesn't stop us. Grabbing my hips to steady us both, Duncan slides the full, hard length of his glorious cock inside me, making a kaleidoscope of bright fireworks explode in my mind, pleasure ripping through my body.

This is all for her.

The feeling of sinking deep into Crystal's body is unlike anything I could have hoped for. It's so, so much better than anything I let run through my head on those long and lonely nights out in the wilderness. I can smell her all around me, and when I breathe in, it's something so fresh and new that we may as well have been together for the first time right here on the bathroom floor of her house in the middle of a hurricane.

The energy outside has nothing on the power I feel between us. This is what I was waiting for. This is what I wanted to come home to. This is *right*.

I can't help but press my lips to hers. There's such a magnetic attraction between us that it couldn't be any other way. I grip her hips as I feel her soft lips brush up against the rough stubble on my upper lip and around my mouth. I feel her let out a soft sigh of both frustration and delight as I start to rock into her.

This is everything.

I've spent the past four years going out into some of the most dangerous parts of the world, dealing with the most dangerous men known to mankind, taking on missions that have brought me within an inch of my life. And all that time, the one person who's been at the center of my world in my mind, heart, and soul has been Crystal.

I can admit that to myself as I start thrusting into her harder. I put my hand behind her to the small of her back to hold onto her as I get an angle that I can feel her enjoying, every inch of my long, thick shaft filling her up and making her feel warmer by the moment. This is all for her, every bit of it. I enjoy it, of course— I've dreamed of this, hungered for this, even lusted for this. Crystal feels unbelievable. But the real reason for all of it is her.

She deserves everything. Everything I've done is with her in mind, keeping her safe. It's all to build her a better and brighter future in this world full of darkness. And right now, the night is at its blackest, and she needs this comfort.

We can only save Dakota once the tornado passes, and though Jake is not the man I knew him to be, I have to believe that he wouldn't hurt a child. But Crystal needs to be distracted from the worrying thoughts that I know must be spinning in her head.

I put my hands on her thighs and run them up and down as I rock into her. I feel the bulging crown of my cock grinding against her inner depths and pulsing along with me. She clenches and relaxes, feeling me in every part of her that I can reach. I start picking up speed and working her harder. My body's muscles are tight and honed to perfection. I know she admires it, but there is so much more to it than that. It's what it can do for her that matters.

I feel that, and I know she feels it as I lift her hips up and start thrusting harder and faster into her. My body is trained to endure anything, to work with such precision and patience that it can keep going in any way I want it. I maintain it religiously, all for her.

She deserves this and so much more.

The sounds of her gasping as I pound into her over and over again are music to my ears. I grip her hips and thrust my shaft as deep as it will go, grinding the bulging tip against her inner walls and then repeating it all. I feel her trying to writhe under me, but I hold her down so she can't squirm away from the feelings my body is pouring out into her.

We've tasted each other, and it was sweeter than communion for both of us. When I picked her out in high school, I knew what I was doing. I was building something beautiful, and I never wanted that to falter.

I didn't run off to become a Navy SEAL just out of vanity or some kind of childish machismo. I did it so that I could make the world better for her, and part of that was making myself as perfect as possible.

I bend down as I rut into her and take her breast in my mouth. My tongue rolls over the stiff nipple, teasing it and feeling how hard it is. Knowing how much of a response I can get from her body is thrilling, more thrilling than anything I do out in the field. No amount of scaling the manors of crime lords or shots made at nearly a mile away through the scope of a sniper rifle can come close to the feeling of fucking Crystal.

My Crystal.

I slide in and out of her as if gliding over water. She's so wet and slick that nothing stops us from going hard on each other, harder than I've ever gone before. I've been on leave before, and I've had plenty of chances to be with women— good women, wonderful people who are both beautiful and lead rich lives. But I never indulged in that. I knew none could compare to my Crystal. Whether or not she moved on while I was gone, I knew there was never going to be anything that would come near what she meant to me.

Part of why I came back to our hometown was to find closure. I couldn't have just left so much unsaid between us. I had to find out whether it was time to close that chapter of my life or open a new one.

And right now, the chapter we're opening together is such an emotional release that I feel better than I have in years.

I feel my cock pulse as she clenches her tight pussy around me. She shudders in delight as she feels the thick girth of my vein-ribbed cock deep in her, grinding against every inch of her pussy. My balls are swollen and heavy. They slap against her softly every time I buck my hips into her.

I put her ankles up on my shoulders and bend forward, pressing her tight and rutting into her as if driven by pure instinct, nothing but raw need. I look down at her panting, blushing face, and I feel so full of love that I could burst.

It has been so long since I've felt this kind of pure emotion, this unfettered affection for another human being, that I didn't know how starved I was for it— for her, specifically. So many emotions boil within me, like a cocktail of love for Crystal that I'm only just now shaking up to pour into her.

She pushes her hips up in time with me as if our bodies were made knowing each other intimately. She puts her hands on my thighs and drags her nails down them as she sucks in a sharp breath, eyes clenched, her blush growing more intense by the moment. My cock is more stiff and rigid inside her than ever before, and I know that soon, I will release. But I want it to be perfect.

I slow down enough to get her attention, then let her legs fall off my shoulders to kiss her on the lips and smile at her before I slowly pull out. She looks up at me with a pleading, confused face, but I sit back and pick her up, turning her around and facing her away from me so that all I can see is her round ass, curvy body, and that lush hair that I love the feel of so much.

I let her sink down onto my cock, and she lets out a sight of delight as her hands touch the ground. From this new position, I feel the same Crystal in a whole new way, and it's magical. I hold her hips firmly and put my hand around her mouth so that I can attack her neck with my lips, kissing her and grazing the soft skin with my teeth as I start pounding up into her just as fiercely as I did while we were in mating press.

My cock grinds against her g-spot, and I feel her whole body tensing up as I start to drive her closer and closer to release. Her hands go up to her breasts, and she fondles them with a deep, long sigh that ends in a note of a whimper. She needs release as badly as I do.

I bring both hands down to her hips and hold her tight against me as I fuck her, letting go of my inhibitions and unleashing all the energy I've held onto. She puts her hands back on my legs to hold on as I rut into her, cock swollen to its limits and every cell in my body screaming at me to release.

"Fuck," Crystal whimpers, and I can feel that she's so, so close to her own release. I want us to do it together, at the same time. I reach up and grope her breasts, holding onto her and squeezing them and rolling my thumbs over her stiff nipples while I let go of my last shred of rhythm. My rutting gets savage and possessive.

I feel like I'm claiming a war-prize after my long tour of duty, and it couldn't be sweeter.

She draws in a sharp breath just as I feel myself go over the edge. Her fingernails dig into my thighs, and as soon as the first shot of my come bursts up into her, she lets out a squeal of delight as the thunder claps overhead so loud and close that I feel the whole house shake.

Shot after shot of my seed spills into her. It doesn't feel anything like I imagined it. It feels so, so much better. It's a mind-blowing experience, both our bodies coming together. Every nerve in her body is at attention as the orgasm rolls through her body, and I feel like it's connected to mine somehow, on a spiritual level I can't hope to understand. But it's there, and we revel in it for every last second.

When we finally come to an end, I hear one last rumble from the thunder outside, but after that, the sounds of chaos start to fade. We pant, leaning against each other for a few moments more before I speak.

"Crystal...that was unbelievable," my husky voice says. I help her off me slowly, and she turns around to throw her arms around my neck and kiss me. I lean back as she lays on top of me, half-laughing, half moaning as we make out on the floor, her stomach pressed against my cock and coaxing out one last spurt of fluid before I'm empty.

"You're telling me," she purrs before I press my lips to hers. I wait for a moment like that, then smile in the kiss and pull back.

"Hear that?"

"No."

"Exactly," I say, helping her stand up with me. "The storm, it's calmed down. You can still hear the rain, but the tornadoes must have passed— we might have our shot."

Even though we both want desperately to stay and hold each other, to cuddle and catch up on the long years that have passed, we don't hesitate to spring to action. Dakota takes top priority by far. For both of us.

A minute later, we're staggering out of the house, and my jaw drops. The hurricane's tornadoes have ripped a path through the neighborhood, narrowly missing the townhouse. One on the far end of the row wasn't so lucky, but both Crystal's and Jake's seem to be...

Not quite untouched. Crystal screams as she sees a small sedan on its side, halfway inside Jake's house through smashed wood and debris. The wind must have blown it in. She takes off running in that direction, and I barely have time to chase after her.

"Crystal, be careful!" I say as I catch up to her and get ahead of her, slogging through the water and reaching Jake's door. It's hanging open, and I kick it down and storm inside, pulling my gun out and looking around wildly.

There's water all over the floor, along with the front half of the car that got blown into the house. I move through the place, listening for signs of movement, but I hear nothing.

"He's not here," I say finally, looking around.

She wrings her hands, eyes wide, and I can see her already starting to go over terrible thoughts in her mind. I step forward and wrap an arm around her, hugging her close to me. "What if…"

"We don't know anything until we find them," I say firmly, not willing to entertain any apocalyptic thoughts of hers.

"How can we find them? The storm is still going on, this fucking hurricane is endless!" she says, pushing away from me and putting her hands in her hair.

"We look around for context clues in the house," I say. "I can search this place quickly and figure out where he might have gone. Failing that, we know there are only two directions he can really go, and there's a Coast Guard barricade set up near at least one of them. We *will* get to him."

I make my way over to a desk in the kitchen and start rifling through different envelopes, and I hear Crystal walk up behind me, saying nothing. She's quiet for too long, and finally, I turn around to look at her. I expect to see her looking at the floor anxiously, but instead, she's staring at me. There's something on the tip of her tongue, but she's hesitating.

"What is it?" I ask gently, furrowing my brow.

"Duncan," she says weakly, closing her eyes and taking a deep breath. "I... I don't know what's about to happen, so you need to know something. Dakota..."

Everything in my body goes still in that tense split-second that tells me what's about to come out of her mouth before she even says it.

"Dakota is your daughter."

CRYSTAL

*D*uncan stares at me, those beautiful green eyes wide with shock and confusion. My heart is thumping wildly in my chest as I await his response. I have no idea how he will react to this kind of a bombshell being dropped on him.

I mean, I don't even know how *I* would react to such a crazy, life-altering revelation. When I first found out I was pregnant, I kind of lost my mind for a few days. I wandered around in a stupor, totally shell-shocked by the startling news. I had never seen it coming.

Somehow, the idea of getting pregnant never once crossed my mind. Maybe it was because I was just a stupid teenager. Maybe it was because my plans and dreams for the future were so big and so bright that they obscured everything else completely and made me lose my grip on reality for a while. But one thing is for sure, seeing that little blue plus sign on the pregnancy test definitely rocked my world. Nothing will rip you out of your lofty fantasies like a bitter dose of reality. I remembered that there were, in fact, consequences of sleeping with the man of your dreams, and sometimes that consequence was a beautiful, angelic baby girl.

I stare back at Duncan, biting my lip nervously. It was a huge shock to me when I got the news at first, so I can only imagine what must be going through his head. I watch a series of powerful emotions cross over his handsome, angular features. Shock. Wonder. Amazement. Relief. And finally… joy.

He strides over to me, closing the space between us in a couple seconds, and pulls me into his arms, hugging me tight. "She's mine?" he whispers in disbelief.

I nod, my cheek pressed against his strong chest. "Yes. Dakota is your daughter. She's our daughter. You and I… we made her. Together. I'm so sorry I didn't tell you sooner. I just didn't know what to do," I reply softly.

He pets my hair, and I can feel his heart beating hard against my cheek.

"I didn't want to ask. I didn't want to believe… I never imagined I could feel this way about anyone," he murmurs. "Other than you, I mean. Because Crystal, I have never once stopped loving you. I never stopped dreaming about you, about getting back together. In my darkest hours, your face was the bright light that came to me to lift my spirits. When I was afraid, when I felt my lowest, all I had to do was think of you, and the world got a little lighter. For four years I have dreamed about being with you again. I can't believe it. Not only is Crystal Miller back in my arms, but… we have a child together. A gorgeous little girl. It's amazing."

"I'm so relieved," I gush. "All this time, I've had to keep this secret. No one knows who Dakota's father is besides my mom, and I made her swear to never tell a living soul. It's been such a heavy burden, carrying this secret. I feel so light now."

"But one thing I don't understand is why you felt the need to hide this from me," Duncan says, pushing back to look at me. There's an expression of confusion, etched with pain, on his face. It makes my heart ache to see him this way. He's happy, but he's hurt, too. And I'm the reason why. I owe him a full explanation.

"Oh, Duncan. I was stupid. I thought I was doing what was best for you. Remember when we were teenagers, how we used to meet under the bleachers and just talk together for hours and hours?" I remind him. He nods.

"Of course. Those are some of my happiest memories," he replies. "I remember it all."

I smile faintly. "You used to tell me all about your

dreams of running away to save the world. You wanted to fix what was wrong, bring evil to justice. You were so proud, so strong. So set in your path. I was always in awe of you for knowing exactly what you wanted and being so selfless in your desires. Even back then, you were so good at heart. Not an ounce of selfishness in you," I explain.

"I knew you were destined for great things. I had no doubt in my mind that you were going to make the world a safer, better place. And I thought it would be selfish of me to drag you down and anchor you here, to me. I knew you then and I know you now, Duncan. If I had told you about the baby, you would have dropped everything to stay with me. You would have thrown away your beautiful dreams and your service to this country to be a father. But you're meant for so much more than that. I needed you, but the world needed you even more. That's why I never told you. I thought I was doing the right thing."

"I was ambitious, yes, but I was also naive. I thought it would be much easier than it was. I thought I could leave and change the world so quickly. I was wrong. It's much harder than I expected. I'm deeply humbled by my successes as well as my failures. Everything I learned out there in the field only led me back to you, sweetheart. Running away made me realize how desperately I wanted to come back home. And by home, I don't just mean Kitty Hawk. I don't mean the Outer

Banks, and I don't mean North Carolina. I mean you, Crystal. You are my home. Wherever we are together, that's where I ought to be," Duncan tells me earnestly. "I thought I wanted the world, but I learned that, really, all I want is you."

"I want you, too. I always have. And I always will. I'm sorry for trying to ignore my feelings. I should have been honest with you. I can never give you back these four years you've missed, and now… now there's a chance neither of us will ever get a chance to see our daughter again," I burst out crying. Duncan kisses me on the forehead, patting my back.

"I know, I know. It's scary. But you have to have hope, Crystal. You can't give up yet. We are going to find her. I swear," he assures me firmly.

"I should have known. I should have seen this coming," I mumble, sniffling back tears. "Jake said he's been watching me. Watching *us*. How did all of that slip right by me? I always thought my instincts were so good, so accurate. But I never got a bad vibe from him. Not at all. I mean, hell, he was my friend. He was your friend, too!"

"People can be deceptive. Some wolves wear sheep's clothing so they can get within striking distance of the lambs," Duncan says sagely, frowning with anger. I can feel the rage radiating from him, the sense of pure betrayal, even though he manages to keep his voice even-keeled somehow. He has a much better-trained sense of restraint than I do, clearly.

We wander through Jake's house together, painstakingly checking under every item, opening drawers and cabinets, checking each room methodically. When we find anything that looks useful, like a stack of small bills on the table or a heavy-duty flashlight on the kitchen counter, we go ahead and pocket it. I don't feel even the slightest bit guilty for looting Jake's house. He took my daughter, so as far as I'm concerned, he owes me. Everything. When we finally reach Jake's bedroom and push open the door, I clutch my stomach and clap a hand over my mouth at the sickening sight in front of me. Duncan has to grab me to hold me steady as we look around with pure dread.

On the wall over the headboard of his bed, there are close to a hundred Polaroid photos printed and pinned. I am in every single one of them. They're all candid shots, taken from a distance. Some of them show me through the windows of my house, cleaning, cooking, entertaining the kids. Some of them depict me pulling into my driveway in my sedan. Others are of me in the backyard, grilling hot dogs, reading an e-book, or just sunbathing. There are a few from a joyous summer's day when I filled up a little kiddie pool in the backyard for Dakota to splash around in. We're grinning and laughing in the pictures, totally oblivious to the fact that there was a strange man photographing us from afar.

"Jesus," Duncan swears under his breath. "That fucker."

"He really was watching us," I murmur, feeling the bile rise in my throat. I can't walk any closer, like I'm physically repelled from the shrine of photographs. But I also can't seem to look away. Finally, Duncan nudges me gently, leading me away from the shrine toward Jake's clothes dresser. On the dresser, there are many more Polaroids, but this time, to my infinite relief, they don't include me or Dakota. They're photos of a boat on a lake, tied to the docks. There are pictures of what looks like a beach house or a lake house. There is an older couple smiling in many of the photos, and they look enough like Jake for me to presume they're his parents.

"I remember this," Duncan says suddenly, reaching to pick up a photo of the boat. "This is Jake's parents' place down in Nag's Head. Their vacation home. We went there a couple times as teenagers to party. Believe it or not, his folks are genuinely good people. I have no idea how they managed to raise such a shitty son."

"Recessive genes, maybe?" I joke grimly, picking up another photo, this one depicting a big, brick-red truck. It looks like a vintage or antique model, lovingly restored to its former glory. The date scrawled on the back is from this past March.

"He has a truck, apparently," I note, holding out the photo for Duncan to see. He frowns at it, contemplating something.

"Yeah, he was always into antique cars and trucks. He worked as a mechanic with his dad sometimes in high school. Is that picture recent?" he asks.

I nod. "March of this year."

"And do you recognize the location, by chance?" Duncan prods.

I bite my lip, examining the photo. There is a gigantic magnolia tree with its branches reaching down around the truck, almost like a protective embrace. Then it hits me. There's a magnolia tree visible from my yard. Which means...

"This truck might be out back," I shout. He grabs me by the hand, the two of us rushing through the empty, darkened house to the back yard. Through the dense rain, indeed, we can make out the reddish shadow of a big truck. And because Jake's yard is on a steep incline, the truck is on higher ground.

"Do you think..." I trail off, my heart pounding like crazy.

"We might as well try," Duncan says, fishing around in his pocket. He pulls out a jingly, shiny set of keys. "I found this in his underwear drawer. I sure hope it fits the ignition, because otherwise I just touched that motherfucker's boxer briefs for no damn reason."

"Fingers crossed," I mutter breathlessly as we rush out the back door. We run through the heavy rain, getting drenched for the millionth time, and to our relief, one of the keys opens the driver's side door. We both slide in and I scoot down the bench seat while Duncan gets behind the wheel and shuts the door.

"Moment of truth," he sighs, reaching to fit the key in the ignition. At first, it seems to resist, and my heart starts to sink. But then he finagles it around a little, and it slips right in. I gasp with joy as he turns the key and the engine roars to life.

"Holy shit," I gasp.

"Just curious," Duncan mutters, reaching to turn the radio on. I don't expect anything to work, especially in a truck as old as this one. But again, I'm pleasantly surprised. The radio clicks on, and even though it's a little crackly, we manage to make out what the DJ is saying. It's a news update on the hurricane, and I hold my breath as we drink in the new information.

"...folks in the Kitty Hawk area should be long gone by now, headed west to higher ground and safety. Hurricane Bruno is spitting out tornadoes left and right, and the evacuation centers are overflowing with terrified citizens with their children, all struggling to get out of dodge. And that's not all. I have another unfortunate update to share with you all: the bridge on the southside of town has been completely washed out. I repeat, it is completely washed out. Anyone still left in town— and I hope there aren't any— do not proceed to the bridge."

CRYSTAL

"*D*o you know that woman personally?" Duncan asks me, frowning intently out the driver's side window as he presses the brakes slightly, making the truck slow down as it approaches the small, two-story building. The big, beach-driftwood sign out front is painted with bold, playful lettering: Molly Neptune's Stop 'n' Shop. To my surprise, the sign is still clinging to the front of the building, over the entrance, but it is hanging a little crooked, probably from the powerful winds.

"Yeah, I do. I've probably visited that business at least once a week for years. Molly Neptune's is a big local favorite. I don't know if you'd remember that from back in the day. My parents' old house is just down the street from here, so I spent a lot of time in this neighborhood."

"So, we can trust that the woman over there—

Molly, you say— is genuinely flagging us down for help?" Duncan says, squinting through the rain to stare Molly down as she waves her arms over her head frantically. My stomach turns, feeling uneasy at how suspicious he is of these innocent people.

"Of course! What else would she be doing?" I ask, so stunned that I actually back up a little, as though Duncan's paranoia might be contagious. He tosses me a grim smile over his broad shoulder, a flicker of something like apology in his green eyes.

"I'm sorry, Crystal. It's just that— in my line of work, you tend to see some of the worst aspects of humankind imaginable. I'm not as trusting as I used to be. I love my job, and I love the man it has turned me into for the most part, but I have to admit that it's given me a healthy dose of cynicism. I have to be cautious. Especially since I'm out here with the most precious cargo I can possibly imagine," he tells me gently. He reaches across the console to give my hand a squeeze.

"I understand. You're just trying to look out for me. But this time, I can promise you it's not a Jake situation. I may have been wrong about him— hell, we both were— but I swear to you that Miss Molly and her husband are good people. They've known me since I was a toddler. We need to get Kota, but I can't just abandon them if they need help."

Duncan looks at me hard for a moment, and I can feel him thinking it over, sizing me up, weighing the risks and rewards in his head. The truck rolls to a stop just several yards from the front entrance of the Stop 'n' Shop, which is surrounded by knee-deep water. For once, I am grateful for the existence of oversized car tires, with which Jake's pride and joy is equipped. Duncan turns off the engine and pockets the keys before turning to me and shaking his head.

"You stay here for now. I'm going to get out and go see what Molly wants. Okay? You good with that?" he asks, concern etched across his handsome face.

As much as I want to balk and insist on going with him, I know he's right. It's safer for him to try and work this out first before I get out, too. Besides, what help could I possibly offer up in a situation like this? So I simply nod and say, "Just be quick."

"I know, I know. Hang tight. Don't go anywhere," he says quickly as he pops the driver's side door open and slides out, immediately getting soaked up to his calves. It's then that I realize how very tall he is. The water that barely brushes a few inches below his knees is high enough to splash around Molly's linen-pantsed thighs. The middle-aged woman is still waving and shouting hysterically, and she starts jumping up and down when she sees Duncan get out of the truck. I can vaguely hear her yelling something about her husband. Duncan wades through the murky flood waters, holding both hands up in a show of peace and cooperation.

Molly clasps her hands together in front of her chest, and I feel a twinge of pain in my heart to see that her face is streaked with tears, not just rain. Her cheeks are all ruddy and splotchy, and she is visibly trembling, apparent even from way over here in the truck.

"Fuck it," I murmur, cranking the old-fashioned handle to roll down the window a few inches so I can hear better. Rain starts to drip through onto the driver's seat, but oh well. Duncan and I are both soaked already anyway. What's a little more water? I listen closely to the shouted conversation between Duncan and Molly.

"Excuse me, ma'am. Do you have a problem? Do you need help getting to dry land? Are you stuck here?" Duncan asks loudly.

Molly nods, looking frantic. She points back toward the building and shouts, "You can't see it from here, but a tree fell on the back of my house! I-I own this building. The front lower part here is my shop, but the back and top floor are my home. I live here with my husband, Dave! He's—he's trapped back there in the bedroom and I'm too weak to help get him out. Please, please, help me! I'm so worried for his safety!"

"Oh no," I mumble, tears burning in my eyes. "Not Papa Neptune."

But Duncan immediately gives her a firm nod and slips right into business mode. "Take me to him!" he yells through the pouring rain and howling winds.

"Okay! I'll lead you around back," she calls out. The two of them start wading around to the back of the building, out of my sight. Instantly, I feel ten times more anxious, not being able to see them. This new bundle of nerves on top of my worry about Dakota is too much for me. I realize with a jolt that I just cannot be alone right now. I can't be alone with my worries.

I know I said I would wait in the car, but... I just can't. I can't just sit on my hands, with everything out of my control.

So, swearing under my breath at how cold and gross the flood water is, I slide out the driver's side door and start wading across the parking lot. Unlike Duncan, I'm not the approximate height and breadth of a yeti, so the water is above my knees. It feels like moving through molasses, the rushing waters are so difficult to wade through. As I make my way slowly and methodically around back of the Stop 'n' Shop, I can hear Molly crying hysterically, punctuated now and again by a laborious grunt from Duncan. When I turn the corner, I gasp and clap my hands over my mouth.

The sight is even worse than I expected. The back of the building has a small, studio-apartment-sized living space with a screened patio adjoining what must be Molly and Dave's bedroom. There is, in fact, a massive palm tree fallen across the bedroom. The heavy, dense trunk has caused the ceiling to collapse, and the sharp, thick palm fronds have closed down over the bed where Dave is lying trapped. It almost looks as though a set of razor-sharp, gigantic, monstrous teeth are biting down on the bed, Dave pinned beneath them.

"Dave, sweetheart, hold on!" Molly cries out, her shoulders quaking with sobs. Dave's body is mostly obscured by the wreckage of fallen, split beams, debris blown into the chasm by the fierce winds, and chunks of serrated palm fronds. Rain pours into what once was their sweet little bedroom, and it hurts my heart to see the splintered ceiling shattered across the flooded floor.

Water is quickly spilling into the room, mostly rain with the occasional splash of groundwater. Their dresser drawers are hanging open at jaunty angles, the contents within getting pelted with rain and ruined. I even see a few framed portraits floating around in the flotsam. Duncan wades through the water as quickly as he can manage, his powerful body cutting through the dirty flood much more easily than I can. I know there's not much I can do to help Dave, but I desperately want to be of some assistance, somehow, so I decide I can handle Molly.

"Molly, it's alright!" I call out, wading toward her.

She jumps in surprise and whips around, her eyes going wide at the sight of me. Duncan hears me, too, and turns back to grimace at me rather disapprovingly. I mean, I did just defy the *one* instruction he gave me. But to his credit, he quickly returns to the task at hand, making his way through the wreckage to step into the washed-out husk of the Neptunes' bedroom. I hurry over to Molly and drape an arm around her shoulders. Her face crumples into sobs as she turns to fold into my arms, shaking with emotion. I pat her on the back, wishing I could take her worry away.

"I know, I'm sorry. I'm here for you," I tell her softly.

She nods, her soft silver hair plastered to the sides of her head with water. "I just— I couldn't do anything. The storm came so quickly. We didn't have time to evacuate. We were in the process of boarding up the shop when Dave went outside to secure the sign. The winds were so strong and this big chunk of concrete from the construction site down the streets came flying through the air and struck him in the head. He was only bleeding a little, but I think he might have a concussion, so I told him to go lie down in bed while I kept working on the storm preparations. But then... then..." she pauses to sniffle and wipe furiously at her eyes, "I hear this horrible, loud cracking sound. The whole shop shook and you know, it's silly, but my first thought was that it was an earthquake! That's how big it was!"

"And that was the tree falling through the building?" I prompt her.

Molly whimpers, "Yes. It was the stupid tree. I can't believe our bad luck. I mean, come on. We've been finagling with our landscaper guy to get that tree cut down for years, but he kept saying it's too big a job and putting it off. Well, it's down now! And it took my husband down with it!" She bursts into tears again, leaning on me for support while I watch Duncan heroically get to work freeing Dave from underneath the palm tree. To my mild relief, I see Dave moving— he nods his head and reaches out an arm toward Duncan.

"Look, Molly! He's moving. Dave's alive. He's going to be okay, I promise," I insist, hoping to god that I'm right. Molly looks over at the two men and lets out a little yelp of mingled worry and joy.

"Oh, my sweet man! Hold on, Davey!" she cries out, cupping her hand around her mouth.

Dave looks over at us and manages a pained smile, his fingers forming into the OK symbol. Molly smiles through her tears and murmurs, "That's my Davey. Tough as nails. He's survived more hurricanes than anyone. I knew he'd be okay! Who's the hunk, by the way?"

I smile and reply simply, "An old friend. A good one."

"Well, he's a damn lifesaver. Look at him go!" Molly gasps.

Duncan has managed to get his thick arms underneath the broad, rough trunk of the palm tree and is in the process of lifting it. With a straining grunt, he bends at the knees and then pushes up, shoving the tree just far enough to free Dave's body. The older man groans with relief and starts to sit up, even though his bare chest is bruised and bloody from the coarse bark scratching deeply into his flesh. Molly lets go of me and rushes clumsily through the water, crying tears of happiness as she climbs into the rubble and throws her arms around her husband's neck, peppering his face with kisses.

"Come on! We need to get to the front of the building where it's still dry," Duncan shouts. I hurry over to help as we all three support Dave, letting him lean on us as we wade through the water. Up close, his injuries look a little more gruesome, and definitely painful. But Dave doesn't let out so much as a grunt of pain as we help him limp around to the front and through the entrance to the Stop 'n' Shop. By now, Dave can walk pretty well on his own, so Molly and I take over leading him to one of the dining booths near the counter. I can distinctly recall sitting in this exact booth with my father, going to town on fried fish. But right now, it's being smeared with bright red blood, as Dave lurches into the booth and leans his head back against the window, closing his eyes and breathing heavily. I can tell he's doing his best to hide his pain from Molly.

Duncan has jumped into action already, looking around for supplies. "You guys have a first aid kit in here somewhere?" he asks Molly.

Without tearing her eyes away from Dave she replies, "Yes. Behind that counter there. Bottom shelf behind the antiseptic wipes."

"Good," Duncan mutters gruffly.

"Can I help somehow?" I ask. Duncan nods.

"Yeah, you're going to hold one of Dave's hands for me while his wife holds his other hand. Dave, I want you to squeeze. When it hurts, just squeeze. Close your eyes. You probably don't want to look at all the blood. Might make you woozy," he explains as he comes over with a first aid kit.

"I think I'll be okay—auughh!" Dave groans as Duncan dabs at his bloody chest with an alcohol-soaked rag. Molly and I grab for the poor guy's hands and let him squeeze as hard as he needs while Duncan cleans up his wounds. Once the blood is mostly cleared away, it looks a lot better, and I can feel the relief radiating from Molly and Dave.

"You're lucky," Duncan says. "Most of these are very superficial wounds. You're going to be just fine. After I patch this up with bandages, you're probably going to want to wear shirts for a while just to reduce exposure."

"You got it, man. I can't thank you enough,"

Dave says, nodding. Molly dabs gingerly at the sweat beading on her husband's brow, worrying over him like a mother hen. It's really sweet to see that they're still clearly so in love after all these years.

"Don't mention it," Duncan replies. "I'm going to patch up that shattered window by the front now so you two can stay safe 'til the storm ends. Toolbox?"

"Under that same counter," Molly quips.

"Can I help?" I ask again, feeling like a broken record. Duncan stops for a moment and graces me with a roguish, genuine smile.

"No, sweetheart. Not really. You just sit tight and keep the Neptunes company, alright? This won't take me very long," he says softly. I smile and nod.

He gets to work repairing the window and boarding up the rest of the them to prevent more damage. Meanwhile, Molly turns on the store radio so we can all listen in. The newest update is a bad one: that apparently there's a whole new tropical storm gaining traction out in the Atlantic, building up steam and heading straight for the Outer Banks, just like Bruno. Molly heaves a sigh, shaking her head.

"Boy, what did the Outer Banks do to deserve all this?" she laments, leaning her head against Dave's uninjured shoulder. He scoffs.

"We didn't do anything," he grunts. "It's probably one of those billionaire golf club guys who's accrued all kinds of dirty karma, and we just happen to be in the line of fire."

"Spoken like a true hippie," Molly says, stifling a chuckle. It's nice to see that we can all maintain our sense of humor to some degree, even in the face of danger.

Duncan comes marching back over, dusting off his hands on his soaked jeans. "Well, that's all taken care of. Now, I can't promise those boards will hold up completely with this new storm headed our way, but it's better than nothing. Are you two going to try and evacuate before the next one hits?"

Molly and Dave exchange looks of resignation. Dave says sagely, "We wouldn't have anywhere to go. Besides, our car got washed away in the flood. It's probably halfway to Nag's Head by now."

Duncan catches my eye and a wordless exchange passes between us. It's time to get out of here. We have a kidnapper to catch up to and an innocent little girl to rescue. *Our* little girl.

"You're all patched up, so stay safe. We have to go," Duncan says. Molly looks startled.

"Really? Are you sure? It's so dangerous out there. You two ought to stay here with us where at least there's some chance of survival," she protests, laying a hand on my arm. I offer her a smile of gratitude and pat her hand.

"Thank you, but we've got to go. I have— someone to meet," I answer cryptically. I don't want to get into the mess of it now. I don't want Molly to notice that Dakota isn't with us and start asking questions. I don't have time to explain. We just have to go.

"Be careful here, folks," Duncan tells them as he helps me up to leave.

"Hey, you too, man. It's hell out there," Dave says, nodding.

"Thank you so much for stopping. He would have died without you, I couldn't believe I was really seeing someone outside in this mess, I was screaming out there for so long for help. You're an angel," Molly tells Duncan fervently.

He smiles. "No problem. Good to meet you."

"Right back at you, dude," says Davy, who gives us a salute.

Duncan and I make our way to the entrance to leave, my heart already hammering away at the thought of all the time we must have just lost, how much farther away Jake must have absconded with my child. I'm so distracted that at first, I don't notice a new and frightening sound loud enough to be heard over the wind and rain. But at the door, Duncan holds an arm out in front of me, frowning as he peeks through the cracks in the boarded-up glass pane.

The sound is like buzzsaws, only deeper and louder. The noise of it shakes the ground beneath our feet, and slowly my brain deciphers that the sound belongs to the revving of motorcycle engines. "What is it?" I ask nervously, trying to peer over Duncan's shoulder, but I'm far too short to see. He scowls and sighs, his hands curling into fists.

"Bikers," he growls. "A biker gang, by the looks of it. And I don't think they're here to help. Remember those opportunistic predators I told you about? Well, they're here."

DUNCAN

The sound of a shotgun going off outside tells me exactly how willing to negotiate the fuckers outside must be. In an instant, I draw my pistol and grab Crystal, pulling her down and hurrying her behind the counter of the store.

"Get down!" I bark to the others, but I don't even wait for them to respond. I hurry over to the old man and drag him on his improvised stretcher to one of the back rooms while his wife gets down behind the counter with Crystal, then darts in after me to hide with her husband.

"Should have known I'd have to deal with looters sooner or later, but I didn't think they'd turn violent this fast," I grumble as I get the husband situated before turning to his wife. "Ma'am, I need you to stay here and keep down— I'll take care of this."

"O-okay," she says, her voice quaking as she looks between me and the windows with wide eyes. Just as she says that, the sound of a gun going off rings through the building, and bullet holes appear in the wood that's boarding up the windows, followed by debris falling from the ceiling.

"Shit," I curse under my breath as I get down again and make my way to the window. I peek out just enough not to reveal myself and see what we're up against.

At a glance, I count six bikes. Two of them are stopped, holding guns and watching for signs of movement from the shop. If this were any other time where I was just on my own, I wouldn't bother with these punks. I could slip up into the rafters or out the back and wait them out rather than bothering with a fight.

Right now, though? I'm holding down the fort with the mother of my child and two almost-senior citizens, one of whom is injured and needs medical attention. And these guys are firing live ammo at us, and something tells me they aren't interested in hostages. I have no choice.

My training kicks in seamlessly. From behind the window, I take aim with my pistol and line up my shot in the span of about a second.

I fire two shots.

The bikers go down so fast that it takes the other four a second to realize what's just happened. While they're distracted, I move to the opposite side of the building. A moment later, bullet holes start appearing in the wall I was hiding behind, and I hear them cursing and shouting from outside.

"We have to get out of here!" I shout to Crystal.

"We can't leave them!" Crystal shouts back, eyes wide.

"I just took down a couple of them," I call to her. "They're pissed, and the longer we stay here, the more damage they'll do! If we can make it out of here, they'll follow *us* instead of wanting to bother them!" I explain hurriedly with a gesture to Molly and Davey huddled in the back room. Crystal hesitates a moment, and I pop out of cover to fire off one more round at the tire of one of the bikers before dashing over to Crystal.

I take her by the hand, and she yelps as I pull her with me to the stock room where the back door is. The sounds of gunfire keep pattering against the walls of the building as we go, staying low and staying focused. I've led civilians out of hot zones before— I can lead the mother of my daughter to safety from a handful of shits who think we're nothing but weak prey here.

We make it out of the building and race for the truck. I open the driver's side door and nearly push Crystal inside to crawl over the emergency brake to the passenger's seat while I turn to watch her back.

I do so just in time— two of the bikes roar

around the corner of the building, guns out, and before I can even get off a shot, bullets fly toward us. One grazes my leg ever so slightly, enough to sting but not to put me down, and the other takes out a headlight on the truck. I fire two more rounds at them blindly, but even so, I hear one of them grunt in pain as a shot hits his shoulder. The two peel away, giving me just enough time to hop into the car, turn the ignition, and roar away.

"There's four of them on our tail now!" Crystal shouts after looking over her shoulder at the bikes roaring behind us.

"Good," I say without thinking about it.

"The fuck do you mean, 'good'?" she blurts with wide eyes.

"Well," I backpedal, "not 'good' like all around good, but 'good' that they're following us instead of hanging back to pick on the store owners. I don't doubt that Mr. Surfer Hippie has a gun behind the counter, but it's not going to be much help to either of them in this situation. *I*, on the other hand, have more than one gun, and I know how to use it. Speaking of, you still remember that time I took you to the shooting range before I left town, right? When we were eighteen?"

"Yeah," she says, confused.

I hand her my gun as I barrel down the road, swerving to the left just in time to make one of the bikers' bullets ricochet off the side of the car. I then pull up the leg of my soaked denim pants to reveal my spare gun and an extra clip of ammo I have strapped to my calf. I take out the ammo and hand it to her.

"Can you load that for me?" I ask. Without another word, she bites her lip for a moment before hastily loading the pistol, and I'm proud to see that she does it perfectly. It's hard to grow up in North Carolina without knowing your way around a firearm, for better or for worse.

"Don't you have two guns there?" she asks, nodding to my leg.

"I do, but if you can help it, you never want to be in a situation where you have two guns that need reloading," I say, "and a moving truck happens to be very good for that."

"Fair enough," she says.

"Now, hold on," I warn her, seconds before taking a sharp turn into another neighborhood.

Kitty Hawk is usually just a series of beach-style houses lined up street after street, which doesn't provide a lot of cover for a vehicle chase, but it's better than driving in a straight line. I drive Jake's truck through someone's yard, ploughing right through a spread of tacky lawn ornaments and through a half-smashed fence into a muddy back-yard. The bikers barrel in after me, guns out.

"Get down!" I order, and she obeys, covering her head and bending over as far as she can go. I pull the handbrake and skid around, spraying up a small wave of mud that cakes the bikers chasing after us. They all come to screeching halts, which is a perfect distraction I use to pull off and leave them in the dust.

What I don't expect is Crystal, who I realize is rolling down the window. Before I can stop her, she fires off two rounds at the bikers, and I see one of their headlights pop, scaring one of the bikers shitless.

"Fuckers," she mutters after I yank her back inside.

"What were you thinking?" I say as I drive us on the bumpy ride across yard after yard, swerving to avoid an upside-down above-ground pool and someone's pontoon boat that's lying against some poor homeowner's newly smashed porch. "You could have gotten hurt!"

"They're shooting at the man I love, too," she says, "you bet your ass I'll take a few pot shots at them!"

I open my mouth to protest, but I can't help but smile as we pull out onto the road. Glancing in the rear-view mirror, I see that the bikers are still after us, and I frown.

"We can't keep this up all the way to where Jake is," I say. "If the noise doesn't tip him off, the firefight I'm going to have to have with these assholes is going to give him all the time he needs to get further away."

"You're right," Crystal murmurs. "Any ideas?"

"Yeah, I've got one," I say, nodding up ahead, and Crystal follows my gaze... and her jaw drops. The skies up ahead are pitch-black clouds, rippling with electricity, and the thunder starts to roll so deep and loud that we can feel it in the seat of the moving truck.

A bullet takes out the side mirror on my side of the car, and I curse, taking the gun from Crystal's hand and firing back at the bikers. To my surprise, I see one of them spin out, his front tire hit by one of my bullets. The three remaining don't go back for him. They're out for blood.

The wind starts to howl so intensely that the truck shakes, and I see a bandana from one of the bikers get blown off.

"Think the storm will shake them?" Crystal asks anxiously. "I mean, we're not going to be much better off."

"No, but we have cover. They don't," I say. "While the storm was raging earlier, you can bet they were cowering in someone's house waiting the storm out. If we can get them far enough into the storm, they'll be forced to take cover somewhere else, which will both keep them off our ass and keep them from just going back to the store before the Coast Guard can get to the-"

Before I can finish, lightning strikes the ground just ahead of us. I don't stop driving. I can't, even as Crystal lets out a cry of terror before clapping her hands over her mouth.

Stopping means death, but is pressing onward any safer?

CRYSTAL

"*Duncan!*" I cry out in pure terror, instinctively reaching to grasp the edge of the bench seat. I grit my teeth and pull a full-body flinch, as though folding in on myself could possibly protect me from the wrath of the storm raging on outside. It hits me how silly it is that I automatically feel safer in the truck. It's not like these steel panels and glass windows are supernaturally powerful or anything. This isn't a fortress. If the wild, angry elements outside want to reach us… they will.

A crackling bolt of lightning strikes the ground sharply just several yards beyond the front bumper of Jake's truck, a burst of white-hot light exploding in front of us. Sparks go flying in a haze of illumination. The sight is so simultaneously stunning and horrifying that it sends my thoughts spinning back in time, dredging up a memory I have not taken out and dusted off in probably years. In the span of a few seconds, I am hurled into the past, where the world seems to expand and fill those few seconds with all the potency of deja vu.

I can remember standing in the backyard at my parents' modest little bungalow across town, mere streets away from the beach. I was fifteen, stuck dead in the middle of a wash of growing pains. I was tall for my age then and gawky as hell, with my long, skinny arms and my knobbly knees. I was standing under the trees in our yard, listening to the wind softly ruffling through the pine branches. It was evening at the start of autumn, that wistful time of year when there's just a different but indescribable newness to the air. It tastes different. It smells different.

I was standing there with tears streaming down my face, because it was the third anniversary of my father's death. I missed him, and I missed having someone strong like him in my life to build me up and brush off the mean comments I heard from my classmates about how scrawny I was or how goofy I looked in my oversized, outdated hand-me-down clothing from my mom's wardrobe. I had slipped out the back door to cry in peace, away from my mother who was grieving in her own quiet way. I recall wanting desperately to hide my sadness from her. I didn't want her to feel my pain on top of hers. But I also needed support, and had no idea how to ask for it. But then I looked up at the night sky and saw something magical: a meteor shower. So bright and glittering that at first I had to blink and rub my eyes to know that it was real. In that moment, I was distracted away from my pain by a thing of great beauty. Seeing those lights dance across the velvety black sky reminded me that I was very small and the world was very large, and even though I felt so heartbroken at the time, I realized that somewhere under the same exact sky, there were people smiling and laughing and moving on with life. I wanted so badly to join them. To be happy and free again. And for the first time in a long time, I felt like maybe, just maybe, that was possible for me. Despite everything.

I'm jolted back to the present moment when Duncan hisses through gritted teeth, "Hold on tight, sweetheart. This is about to get a little rough."

He grabs the steering wheel with both hands, his knuckles going white with tension, and yanks the wheel hard to the left. The wheels splutter and skid over the watery street, the front-heavy truck losing traction. The bed of the truck spins out in a fan shape as we curl out of the way. Duncan's expert reflexes and driving acumen just barely allow us to dodge the falling telephone pole to the right. I turn and stare wide-eyed out the window to see that the lightning has split the wooden pole nearly in two, a deep, jagged vivisection cracking down from the top to the bottom. There's a sickening, deep rumble that makes the earth quiver and sends violent ripples across the surface of the flood water, and then I see the pole start to actually cleave in half, the remaining part still standing now beginning to fall, too. This is the part attached to the rope-like electrical wires. The black cords swing like a cowboy's lasso in the powerful wind. It reminds me of a bull whip from some Saturday morning cartoon, only much more dangerous, especially as the wires whip around the split pole and start to fall down toward the flooded street.

I whirl around to look out the back windshield at the biker gang. That lightning-struck pole has fallen down like a boundary separating our truck from the angry-looking troublemakers. I can't hear their voices over the combined din of the vehicle engines, the thunder, the rain, and the rushing of my own blood in my ears as my heart pounds, but I can see their terrified faces. I watch their angry, almost smug looks of determination fade to pale panic. The group of them are rumbling up as fast as they can in their pursuit of us, only to slam on the brakes when they notice the electrical wires about to cross their path.

The shriek of tires squealing and skidding on the road fills the air. The front three bikers do their best to rear back and avoid being struck by the heavy cords of electric current, but evidently these guys are more accustomed to slamming the gas pedal than the brakes, because two of them go toppling off their bikes, sending the motorcycles careening across the road in the opposite direction. They flip over into a ditch, the thick wheels spinning and the engines whirring angrily. The second tier of bikers have about a split second to stop before trampling the bodies of their fallen lackeys, and only one of them is successful.

"Oh my god," I gasp, whipping around to face the front, my eyes bugging out of my head with horror. I couldn't turn away quite fast enough to totally avoid seeing the spray of blood across the slick pavement, staining the flood waters pink as human bodies collide with fiery steel and glass. Duncan slams his foot down on the gas pedal, the tires spinning and kicking up splashes of filthy water as the old truck struggles to gain traction and get away.

"Don't look back, babe," Duncan growls, glancing over at me with fierce eyes. "It's about to get much worse back there."

I know he's right. It's good advice. I don't need the mental images to haunt me for the rest of my life. I know people are dying back there. Human beings with lives, with families, friends, hopes, dreams— sure, they're a bunch of semi-murderous looters all bearing a massive chip on their shoulders, but none of that makes it any easier for me to face their deaths. And when the electrical wires finally smack the wet streets with a spine-tingling

ZAP, my heart nearly stops. There's a burst of light behind us, and even through the loudness of the rain and thunder, I can make out the agonized screams of our pursuers, stopped in their tracks and electrocuted by the deadly union of electricity and water.

I can't help it. Pure human curiosity and maybe just a healthy dose of morbid fascination urges me to turn back and look behind us. Luckily, at exactly that moment, the truck tires quit hydroplaning and we skid down the road at top speed, the engine roaring as Duncan feeds it gasoline. The horrific scene behind us is obscured by the pelting rain and lack of light from the sky. The sun is somewhere hidden behind the ominous black clouds, but I can sense that it is setting, slipping away beyond the horizon and plunging the uncertain, waterlogged world of the Outer Banks into eerie darkness.

I turn around in my seat and face forward again, and it takes me a full minute to realize that I'm hyperventilating. My chest aches, my lungs expanding and contracting rapidly while I struggle with every gasping breath. Duncan looks over at me with deep concern on his angular features, and he reaches across to squeeze my thigh.

"Are you okay, sweetheart? Breathe, Crystal. Slowly. In through the nose, out through the mouth. Deep breaths. You're going to be fine. We're going to get through this," he says calmly.

I shake my head, tears burning in my eyes as my chest rises and falls violently.

"I-I can't. I can't handle it. My daughter— Jake— and all those people. Oh god. I'm going to pass out," I murmur breathlessly.

"Stay with me, honey," he urges me, fumbling to grab my hand. "Squeeze my hand, if you can. Just hold on. They can't follow us anymore."

"They—they're dead," I whimper as a tear rolls down my cheek. "I've never seen anything like that before. It all happened so quickly."

"I know," he sighs heavily, staring straight ahead. He's somehow managing to comfort me at the same time as he's expertly dodging obstacles and dips in the road filled with murky water. He's up on the median now, plowing through what once were daisies and overgrown weeds. The median is on slightly higher ground, but I know we're still riding along the knife's edge between survival and death. It's all so much to take in, and with every breath I draw, my mind goes rushing back to Dakota. To my baby. I don't know where she is, not really. For all I know, Jake could have abandoned her somewhere along the Croatan Highway. Or the two of them could have fallen into a ravine or drowned in the flood or sieged by looters or—

"Stop," Duncan says suddenly. "Stop thinking about it. I can feel those cogs turning in your head, Crystal, and I know you're going to a very dark place. You can't do that. Not if we want to survive this disaster."

"I don't know how to think about anything else," I choke out, wiping my eyes.

"It's hard, but you've got to focus on the moment. Stay with me. We will get out of this and we will find your— our daughter. But we'll have to go at it a step at a time," Duncan reminds me wisely. Just then, a few more cracks of lightning streak right on either side of the truck, making me scream and duck down as if someone is firing a gun at us.

"Fuck this," Duncan grunts, grabbing the wheel and whipping it to the right. We go careening across the flooded road, and for a second it feels like we might just start floating, but he's worked up enough momentum to propel us across to the other side. He drives the truck off the road and down a winding, long driveway with a carport.

"Where the hell are we going? Whose house is this?" I demand to know, confused.

"Who knows," Duncan growls, "but it's our place now."

"But what about Dakota?" I protest, staring at him like he's lost his mind.

"Look around, Crystal. The lightning is getting out of hand. It's not safe for us to stay on the road. That will only increase our chances of being electrocuted like those asshole bikers back there. We don't want that. We want to wait this out and survive so we can get back on the road to find Dakota and rip Jake from limb to limb," he explains as we roll down the long drive to the house at the end. It's on a bit of an incline, which will work to our advantage. The place looks as though it's been abandoned in the storm, and I realize it's probably because it belongs to a wealthy person. They always manage to get out first, as they have the money to charter private jets and the freedom to leave work early with less worry about missing hours. The house is two stories, and looks to be about double the square footage of my cozy townhouse. There's a carport out front, which Duncan whips the truck into just as another clap of lightning strikes the ground just several yards away.

"Come with me," he commands, sliding out of the truck and grabbing hold of me to swing me down to the wet concrete. I can feel the static electricity in the air, smell the acrid burn of lightning. With chills erupting all over my body, I follow after Duncan in a numbed sort of trance. He tries to pick the lock for a moment, decides it's a waste of time, and then shoots the doorknob with his smallest gun. Luckily, I hold my hands over my ears just in time to cushion my hearing against the loud bang, and then the door falls open. Duncan grabs my hand and pulls me inside, slamming the door shut and keeping it closed by engaging the deadbolt.

The interior of the house is darkened, the lights evidently burned out, but in the low light I can tell how lushly decorated it is. There are paintings of local scenes and landmarks, and all the furniture looks expertly handmade. Of course, we're not here to appraise the retail value of the place, so Duncan pulls me along until we find a door to— surprisingly — a basement. These are not super common this close to the shore, but this house seems to have been specifically tricked out with all the extras. He hurries to open the door to lead me down the steep staircase, the two of us descending into darkness.

DUNCAN

I bar the basement doors shut behind us as Crystal hurries down inside.

"Hello?" I hear her call as she steps into the basement, and I turn to follow her down to the sound of the doors shuddering violently across the house with another gust of wind. My hair is blown so out of control that I feel my skin stinging from the wind, and Crystal is still trying to smooth her hair out as she inspects the place.

I follow her down to find that we've picked a good place to ride out this part of the storm. It looks like someone's personal space for...drawing. As we step into the basement proper, we see cute little sketches all over the walls, most black and white, some colored in with various kinds of paint. Most of the drawings depict scenes from around the local area. I recognize a few beautiful scenes of the vegetation and the beach, one of the bridge leading to the mainland, and a couple of the airport.

"Someone really likes living around here," Crystal says with raised eyebrows. "Hello? Is anyone here?" she calls out again, but she's answered only with the echo of her own voice.

"I think we're alone," I say as I follow her in. "The basement doors would have been locked if anyone was down here to ride out the storm, and there were no cars outside the house. Granted, the cars could have been blown away," I add, scratching the back of my neck.

"No, I think you're right," she says as she finishes doing a round of the place. There's a couch and a small coffee table, as well as a desk where the owner of this place probably carries out his or her hobby. Hell, these are good enough that they could be professional.

There's also a radio sitting on the studio desk, but it's just crackling softly with no signal. I turn the volume dial down so that the sound is just background noise, and I look around the place with raised eyebrows.

"Pretty damn cozy, if I do say so myself," I say. "I'll have to keep this setup in mind if I ever build my own place."

"Drawing? You?" she asks, smiling with sparkling eyes. "I never imagined you'd be the type."

"You have a lot of time on your hands on long

flights," I say, shrugging and trying not to smile. "I don't pretend I'm any good, but it passes the time."

That's partly a lie. Some of the other guys have said I do good work, and one of them even asked me to draw something he eventually plans to get done as a tattoo. But now probably isn't the best time to talk about the alternate universe where I try to hack it as a freelance artist instead of joining the Navy.

"So, what now?" she asks, flopping down on the couch. "I can't hear much down here. How are we supposed to know when the storm passes?"

"Well, I don't expect us to stay here until the whole hurricane moves over," I say, frowning and approaching her. "Just until this bad spell passes and gives us enough of a break to keep chasing Jake. He's panicky and knows we're after him, most likely, so he'll be running as fast as he can as much as he can until he hits his parents' place."

She nods as I reach the couch, and I slowly sit down next to her. Almost on instinct for both of us, I wrap my arm around her, and she snuggles in close, putting her head against my chest and wrapping her arms around my torso.

"Did we do the right thing? I feel like... my instincts just want me to keep going. Keep chasing Dakota until I find her again. I don't know what he's doing—"

"Shh, shh. He's trying to get you to chase him.

He… If he wants you, he's not going to hurt her. He's using her as bait."

"But he has such a lead on us now. We stopped for Molly—"

"To save her husband's life, Crystal. Could you have lived with yourself if we just ignored them?"

"Can I live with myself if something happens to Dakota because we stopped?"

I sigh, stroking her hair softly.

"I know it's hard to react tactically when something so personal is on the line. So many times in the field, I've had to face the choice of doing what comes naturally by instinct, and just… overriding it to do the thing I know will give us the best chance of success. We've done what I think will give us the best chance of getting Dakota back safe. That's what matters. Instincts… They're good to listen to, but they're not always smart. If you'd gone out in the tornado, you could have gotten blown away, injured, even killed. If we'd rushed this, so much could have gone wrong, and that just puts Dakota in more danger."

"Hey," she says softly after a few moments of silence. "This is…easily one of the worst days of my life, but…it would be a hell of a lot worse if you weren't here."

"I'll take that," I say, chuckling.

"I mean it," she says with a soft smile, and she looks up at me with those crystal-blue eyes so full of love and meaning. "I'm glad you're here, Duncan. I can't possibly tell you enough how screwed I'd be without you."

"I appreciate it, but don't think of it that way," I assure her, giving her a squeeze. "You're an unbelievably capable woman, Crystal. You raised a child on your own— an amazing kid, it sounds like. That's more than I can say."

"Are you kidding? There are literally like, what, thirty? Forty people in the whole world who can say they do what you do?"

"None of what I do includes parenting," I say, laughing, and I feel proud that it earns a smile from her pretty face. "At least, not yet." The words come as a surprise from me as much as they are for Crystal. "I mean…"

"I hadn't really thought about that either," she says softly. "Not that it sounds bad— I mean…" She trails off the same way I did, and we smile at each other in silence. We both know there will be time to talk about that later. For now, though, it's just us, a storm, and a crisis. That's more than enough for us both to handle.

And our hearts are still pounding from the thrill of the chase.

I've been in a lot of fights like that over the years, but all the while, I've never been in one where I can act on the feelings I have afterward when Crystal is on my mind. Now, though, she's right in front of me, and I can tell by the look in her eyes that she's having the same thoughts as I am.

I lean in and kiss her.

It's explosive. The thrill of touching another person like this after so much adrenaline courses through your veins has no comparison. Her hands go to my stubble-ridden face, while mine go to her curvy hips, and I squeeze her, savoring the feel of her body in my grasp. My cock swells hard at the mere feeling of her, but there's so much more to the storm of emotions I feel with her pressed against me.

I take in her scent, the taste of her on my lips, the feeling of her body heat— all of it makes me feel so whole and fulfilled that I don't know how I resisted it for these four long years alone I had out there.

Her hand moves around to the back of my neck, and she feels the short hair on my head as I slide one of my hands around to her back. It wanders up her shirt, feeling her smooth backside before reaching her bra and unhooking it. As soon as it's free, I help her pull her shirt and bra off entirely, and I look at her with a hungry gaze.

My shirt comes off next, giving her a view of my naked chest that makes her blush. It gives me pride to know all the hard work I've put into it pays off in a better way than I ever could have imagined when I was doing endless pull-ups and crunches in training.

Maintaining my body is a way of life, and it's not

one that I'll ever put down— especially not when Crystal looks at me like that.

I descend on her, pinning her between me and the couch as my hands go to her chest and my mouth goes to her neck. I tease the soft skin and lavish it with attention, hearing the moans coming from her as I electrify her body with my touch. I bite her neck gently as we grind against each other on the couch. Her thigh feels my cock pressed against it so that she can know what kind of effect she has on me. I control her exactly as much as I want, steering her hips on the couch and positioning her legs wherever I please.

I unbutton her pants and help her out of them, leaving her naked before me. In short order, I strip the rest of my body too, leaving all our clothes and gear in a pile before the couch. My cock is stiff and bulging for her, and when she wraps her hand around it and starts stroking it up and down, it feels like heaven.

"You have no idea how much I missed this," she says in a tone heavy with desire. I reach down and stroke her hair, staring into her eyes as the golden locks thread around my fingers.

"Every night I was alone," I say, "I wished you were at my side. Sometimes, I even dreamed about it. It was so vivid. I felt like you were there, somehow." I don't know why I'm telling her this, or maybe I do. I don't know. I've spent the past four years suppressing my emotions, being trained to be as machine-like as possible, only following orders and being able to make tactical decisions.

But all that repression only made my love for Crystal grow stronger. It's proof that I won't be able to keep up the military life forever— a lover's heart is beating too strong inside me. And when someone like Crystal is right here in front of me reminding me of that, it's all the more overwhelming.

I fall upon her again, holding her close to me and exploring her body with my hands. My cock rests against her lips. She's already wet. I let it slide back and forth against the outside of it, and she moans, shivering under the sensation rippling through her whole body.

"There were so many nights here where all I could think about was you," she whispers as I kiss her neck. "You were like a ghost, but you were right there with me all along."

I start grinding against her pussy almost on impulse, hips moving back and forth with nothing but pure desire driving me. It simply feels *good* to be so close to her like this, naked on a couch, exploring each other and enjoying the feeling of each other's bodies. I feel my cock pulse, and I let out a husky groan. Her soft body is so irresistible that it makes my head spin.

"We might not have much time," I growl into her ear. "I need to be in you. Now."

My primal lust seems to excite her, and she nods her head quickly.

"On your knees," I order her, and she obeys, turning around and resting her arms on the arm of the couch while looking back at me as she arches her back to show me her ass.

She treats me to such a sight that I feel like I'm looking at her for the first time again. Her round ass points up at me, wet pussy tempting me beyond my control. I reach out and run my hands up and down her curves, letting out another groan of pure desire before I kneel on the couch and position myself just the way I want to.

The next moment, I thrust into her.

Instantly, she draws a sharp breath and lets out a squeak in surprise as the bulging, swollen crown of my cock fills her up and slides through her hot, wet pussy, all along the front of her inner walls and tormenting her g-spot. I start rocking back and forth, relentlessly assaulting that spot as I take hold of her hips and find a good grip.

I start bucking into her immediately. My arms and hips work together like a refined machine, powerful thighs holding me up as I dig into the couch and pound her against it. My balls are swollen and in desperate need of release. They felt just like I did that night at the graduation party, when I fucked Crystal so hard I put a baby into her. This feels like that, so right, so primal and good. I want more of this, as much as I can get.

The way I want Crystal is something I've thought of so much. Our skin gets hot as we fuck on the couch, every new thrust bringing waves of heat rippling through my body. It wells up in my shaft, and every few thrusts, I feel my shaft pulse from the thick midsection to the base, then up through my body. Tension is leaving me in droves.

I am used to feeling powerful. I'm not the kind of man who brags, but my training has made me into the kind of human being who can survive anything Mother Nature can throw at him, as well as just about anything that could happen in a hand-to-hand fight. All the while, though, I remember to stay humble, to know that I can falter just like anyone else.

Being inside Crystal is different.

She makes me feel invincible.

My tight, virile balls swing under us as I rut into her faster and faster. I can hear her panting, leaning against the couch's arm and arching her back as best as she can as she takes it. The more we wear each other out, the better it feels. The adrenaline pumping through our veins makes this feel like pure bliss, and there's no end in sight.

There's a feeling that comes over me when I've found just the right spot to buck into her, just the perfect way to make her knees go weak and her mouth fall open. When I find it, I tighten my grip on her hips and start going at it relentlessly, and that primal, base desire to keep pounding like that touches on something so pure and bestial inside me that neither of us can stop.

I feel her whole body starting to tense up, and knowing she's about to come makes me go at her all the harder— but I'm not anywhere near my own release. She tries to let out a cry, but her voice cracks, and the faintest sliver of a squeak escapes her before her whole body melts and trembles as the orgasm devastates her. She collapses against the arm of the couch, and I slow down my rutting as I feel her pussy pulse around my cock.

I slowly slide out of her and flip her limp body over to let her look up at me with that blushing face.

She murmurs something I can barely understand, somewhere between a word and a sigh of satisfaction, and I chuckle as I lean down to her and kiss her. I'm expecting her to be entirely limp and exhausted, but as soon as my lips are on her, she wraps her arms around my neck and leans up into the kiss, groaning in pure desire as our tongues dance together.

I grab her hips, and she wraps her legs around mine, pushing her hips up as if begging for more. Still locked in a deep, fierce kiss, I bring my hips back and slide the tip of my cock into her pussy again.

She lets out a single whimper of anticipation before I thrust into her.

The ragged, heady sigh she lets out tells me everything I need to know. I pick up her left leg and drape it over my left shoulder, angling her away from the back of the couch as I scoop her half off the couch. She clings to the arm, still, like a support beam, and her eyes go down to the sight of my thick shaft impaling her pussy.

She was already blushing, but with her eyes locked onto that, she looks like she's just run a marathon. I waste no time in picking up the pace again, and this time, I use one hand to hold her up while another hand goes to her breast. One of her hands goes to the other, and soon, she has to let her head fall back on the arm of the couch to revel in the pure, unrestrained feeling I'm lavishing her with.

My hips pick up pace and start getting piston-like again, ramming into her and feeling the parts of her I've learned to give attention to. Her body speaks to me, and if I listen, I can reward it just the way she deserves. I want to give her everything, let her feel everything, fulfill her in this part of her life in every way that I can.

I lose myself in the softness of her ass and everything about her— her scent, the sound of her moaning voice, everything. I would go on forever if I didn't feel her start to tense up again under me. This time, I know I have to finish with her.

This devastating storm is just about the only thing on the planet that could hope to tear us apart when we want to be with each other, and even so, it isn't doing a very good job of it.

My whole body starts to well up with desire and lust as I let myself start to draw closer to release. Crystal's body writhes under me, but I have complete control over her. I hold her still, making her take everything I'm subjecting her to, and the sounds of her gasps become more delighted with each one.

Finally, her mouth falls open, frozen, and I let myself spill over the edge.

My orgasm wells up in me like a storm, and when it releases, it spreads to every muscle of my body, making me feel so fulfilled, warm, and relaxed that I let a ragged groan out from my chest while my cock fills her up completely. Pulse after pulse of my thick, white seed empties into her while she comes. Our bodies twitch and go weak, and soon, we're basking in each other's afterglow.

We stare at each other, panting, glistening with sweat while I'm buried deep inside her.

"I thought I'd never forget what you were like," I whisper down to her in a husky tone, "but you keep surprising me, baby."

She smiles, then gasps as I slide out of her carefully. She's so overwhelmed that she can barely get herself together while we clean ourselves up and get dressed again.

But just as I'm pulling my shirt back on, something catches my attention.

"Coordinates are . . . I repeat, we are in Nag's Head, at the-"

"What the hell is that?" Crystal asks, suddenly terrified, and I know exactly why.

The voice that reached our ears is Jake's.

I look around wildly, ready to kill a man with my bare hands, but my eyes focus on the radio at the far end of the basement. I approach it and start fiddling with the frequency to get a clearer signal before the voice crackles through.

"Again, this is Jake Johnson, I'm a resident at 215 Blue Sound Lane. I have a three-year-old child with me, and we're fleeing an armed and dangerous man. If the Coast Guard is listening, please, send help! We're trapped at our house by the storm!"

Both our jaws have dropped. Jake isn't just fleeing— he's trying to tell the Coast Guard I'm the villain, between the two of us. But there's no way in hell Jake could have expected we'd be listening to the radio when he broadcasted this message. I turn to look at a terrified Crystal, but my face isn't worried. In fact, I have a wicked smile on my face.

Because he just told us two things: exactly where he is, and the fact that he's still on the island.

"We've got him."

CRYSTAL

"We have to go now!" I insist, getting up and hastily pulling on my clothes. I grab my shorts and start pulling them on, limping as I get one leg through the hole and lose my balance. Duncan is still staring at the radio in surprise— well, maybe not surprise so much as rage. His beautiful green eyes, so remarkably similar to our daughter's eyes, are darkened with anger. He's squinting at the radio so intensely that I wonder if somehow Jake can feel it through the airwaves. Like a telepathic punch to the jaw or something.

"Yes. We need to get going," Duncan answers abruptly, standing up and reaching for his clothes. "Don't worry. I am not going to let this fucker get away. And neither will the storm. The stupid asshole must have gotten spooked. I bet he's regretting his actions now; it's got to be even more stressful trying to survive a storm when you have a three-year-old hostage."

"I hate hearing him even mention her," I admit, wrinkling my nose. "The idea of that man touching my daughter, talking to her... it makes me want to be sick."

"I know. It's difficult. But we have to be aware that it's a good thing he mentioned her over the radio. That's a good sign, even if we hate hearing it. That means she is still alive and under his control. In a natural disaster like this, it's all too easy for children to get lost and separated from their guardians," Duncan points out rather morbidly. My stomach lurches.

"Oh god. That's a horrifying thought," I murmur as I fasten my bra clasps. "But I guess you're right. I just hope he hasn't hurt her during the time she's been with him. Oh, my poor baby. She's got to be so scared right now."

"Well, think of it this way: Dakota knows Jake as her neighbor, right?" Duncan asks.

"Yeah," I answer, nodding as I pull my shirt on over my head.

"Then she probably trusts him to some degree. Of course, you and I both know he's a massive creep and a stalker, but Dakota probably doesn't have any idea about that. She's three. She still finds most adults inherently trustworthy. Besides, I bet he's fed her some cockamamie story about you giving him permission to abscond with her," he explains.

I lace up my tennis shoes, shuddering to myself. I can so clearly imagine it: Jake kneeling down to Dakota's level to tell her, *Your mommy said it's okay to trust me.*

It makes me so sick and so angry I could almost scream. But I remind myself to hold onto that rage, save it up to unleash upon the one person who truly deserves my wrath.

Now that we're both fully dressed, Duncan takes me by the hand and we make our way back up the staircase. He finagles the basement door open and we walk back through the ritzy house. There's a strange, unearthly glow radiating through the windows, and I realize that it's the weird combination of the rising moon and lightning. It's growing oddly quiet outside as we make our way through the house, not the constant crash and rumble there was before. Rain is still falling, and I find myself doubly grateful for the truck being under a carport so we don't have to re-soak ourselves, but it's getting softer by the minute. As we climb into the bench seat of the vintage truck, Duncan looks around with a stony face.

"What is it?" I ask, trying to hold back my impatience. I wanted to get a move on before Jake could have a chance to change his mind and get back on the road with my daughter.

"I think the eye of the storm is passing over," he replies quietly.

My heart skips a beat. "Oh. That's not good, is it?"

He shrugs. "It is what it is. For now, it's okay. In fact, we can use this to our advantage. It will be easier to get to our destination as long as we move quickly," he says, turning the ignition so that the slightly waterlogged engine coughs back to life. He backs the truck out, pulls a tight turnaround, and the truck goes barreling down the long driveway toward the road. I hold onto the edge of the seat with one hand and reach over to grab Duncan's hand with my other. The truck rumbles over the gravel and skids onto the highway, which is still flooded, but hasn't gotten much worse, at least.

We ride along for a while in silence as my mind races in wild directions. All I can think about is Kota. I imagine her shivering and soaked down to the bone, her curly blonde hair plastered down on her head, her big green eyes full of fear. Jake doesn't know how to care for a child. I doubt he knows how to care for anyone or anything, actually. He's a bad man, and I can't wait to scoop my baby out of his evil grasp.

"It's not far from here," I remark, feeling my insides squirm at the thought of actually confronting Jake. Before I can stop myself, the words on my mind come falling out. "Duncan, what if Jake has a weapon?"

Duncan gives my hand a squeeze. "We'll figure it out. I promise. I have dealt with much more dangerous men than Jake Johnson."

I nod, still biting my lip nervously. Then, just before my mind can zone out into worry again, Duncan slams on the brakes and the truck hydroplanes several feet. I cry out in fear and grasp at the seat, confused as to what's going on. Then I crane my neck and look over the front of the truck to see that the road is almost totally washed out by a fast-rushing pool of flood water. It looks deep enough to swim in. My heart plummets.

"Oh my god," I mutter. "What do we do?"

Duncan looks contemplative, a muscle in his jaw twitching. "We have to cross somehow," he says. "This is the only way. And we're so close. We can't turn around and go searching for another route now."

"But how? The water is so deep," I emphasize anxiously.

"I know. And there's no way the truck can get through these waters," he agrees. "That water will destroy this truck. But luckily, it belongs to Jake, so I don't give a damn if it sinks or not. All that matters to me is getting as far as we can. So, here's what we're going to do..."

He opens the driver side and steps out into the

shallower part of the water, where the murky water nearly rises up to his thighs. He gestures for me to come sliding out. "What am I doing?" I ask as he reaches for me. Duncan scoops me into his arms, carrying me like a princess around to the back of the truck. He gently lifts me up into the bed of the truck.

"You stay here. I'm going to try and float us across the best I can," he says, wading back to get into the cabin of the truck. He cranks both the side windows down and revs the engine, rolling the truck forward into the deeper, filthy water. The engine splutters and whines, but Duncan doesn't let up on the gas. Adrenaline is pumping through my veins as we begin the trek across. It's only about twenty or thirty feet, but I know that trying to swim our way across would be fraught with danger, not to mention the fact that it would take us a long time. There's an identifiable current washing to the right, and it would be difficult to fight that.

I hold my breath while the truck begins to give out. I realize with a sinking feeling that we're only just barely more than halfway across— and then the engine promptly dies. The truck is now just floating, at the mercy of the current.

"Shit," I mumble, looking through the back window of the truck cabin to see what Duncan is doing. The truck is starting to sink even more now, the front end lower in the water while the bed pokes up. Duncan immediately squeezes his bulky, powerful body through the open window, swimming out into the flood waters. It's just deep enough that his feet can barely brush the bottom. He swims around back to get me, grabbing a plank of soggy wood floating by and extending it to me.

"Grab hold!" he shouts. "I'm going to get us across."

I hesitate, nervous to put my whole body in the water. But I know I have no choice. So I grasp the plank with both hands, stepping out of the bed of the truck and into the cold, dirty water. I let out a gasp as the icy water rises to my bare arms, goosebumps prickling up on my skin. Duncan begins a combination of swimming and pushing himself along with the tips of his toes, dragging me along behind him, using the plank like a life preserver. All sorts of debris floats around us, some of it sharp and dangerous. There are entire chunks of pavement and asphalt drifting by, a testament to the storm's immense power. I can scarcely breathe as we cross the water, but to my amazement, Duncan manages to get us across.

Gradually, the water becomes shallower, until finally we can both stand easily. I let go of the plank and we walk out of the washed-out ravine hand-in-hand. Up ahead of us, just a block or two down, is the address we need. My heart skips a beat as it dawns on me that the house where Jake is hiding, the Nag's Head home from those Polaroids, is within walking distance. I only wish I knew exactly what we could expect to find there.

As though he can read my mind, Duncan squeezes my hand and says firmly, "We can handle this. Crystal, we are going to get our daughter back. We're almost there."

I've never sprinted faster in my life.

Knowing the goal is in sight, knowing my girl could be behind that door, nothing in the world could stop me from barreling forward through water, across sharp and rusty debris, and anything else in my way to get to the front door of this damn manor. I came back to my hometown to see my girl, but now, I'm here to protect *both* of them.

I reach the front door, and without even breaking my pace, I put my full weight behind a kick that sends the wood flying open with a few splinters scattering in front of me. My gun is already out and at the ready, and my heart is pounding harder than all the times I've burst into the houses of men far more dangerous than Jake.

This isn't about Jake and how dangerous he is.

This is about the vulnerable little life he has in his power.

The inside of the house is what I would expect from a family as wealthy as Jake's. I'd spent time with him in high school, so I know how his family lives, but I've never been to this place. It must be newer. The furniture, the art on the walls, the quality of the tile floors, it all speaks to wealth.

It isn't fashionable. I never grew up with an eye for that kind of thing, but over the years of my service, I've raided manors of the rich who both do and don't have taste, and I know what good taste looks like. This isn't it.

The outside of the house shows some damage, but the interior is eerily untouched. After everything I've seen today, it feels wrong to be standing somewhere that has been spared the onslaught of the storm, especially knowing the kind of person who's using this place.

I move forward slowly, keeping my gun up and ears open. Jake isn't a man who knows how to fight, unless he's changed dramatically over the years, but that doesn't make him much less dangerous. The element of surprise means everything. I've watched trained men and women get blindsided by people who can barely hold a gun, just because they happened to get the drop on them.

I move through the living room, where a Persian rug lies on the floor contrasting sharply with the tacky sofa and loveseat that looks like it could have come out of my great aunt's house— no offense to her memory. I hear nothing but the sounds of Crystal's footsteps behind me as she staggers into the house.

I hold up a hand to signal that we need to keep quiet, and she nods, eyes wide and quivering. The main room of the house is an open concept living room that exposes a counter dividing it from the kitchen. Both are empty, but beyond the kitchen is a hallway leading into darkness.

I approach the hallway slowly, and on the counter nearest to it, I notice a glass with light yellow liquid in it next to a bottle of rum. There are two ice cubes melting in the glass of rum. Every nerve in my body is poised— he was here recently, and he's almost certainly still in the building.

Crystal walks up behind me, keeping some distance as I move toward the hallway.

Then, a voice.

"...Mommy?"

It's Dakota, and she sounds scared, just on the verge of tears, probably just as terrified by the sound of me kicking down the door as by everything that's been happening to her the past few hours.

I hear Crystal draw in a sharp breath, but I hold out my arm behind me just in case she follows her instinct to dart into the room to get her baby. I don't blame her for that instinct for one second— I feel it too. It's every parent's instinct to do everything possible to protect the child. But Jake might well know that, and he might be using that to his advantage against us. For all I know, he could be waiting just around the corner with a loaded gun. I can't take that chance, for all our sakes.

So, I pick up the bottle of rum from the counter silently, then toss it down the hallway at about chest-level to provoke a reaction from Jake if he's standing in the darkness, waiting for me to come into view.

The rum bottle clatters to the ground loudly, but as it rolls, I don't hear the sound of any adult man making a move.

I advance slowly.

The hallway is full of family photos cast in shadow, none of them looking very happy. I can tell the difference between a real smile and a fake one. But I don't pay much attention to them— the end of the hallway on the left hand side is where my goal is.

There's a door there, open, a faint bit of light filtering through it from a window that must not have even been boarded up. That's where the sound of Dakota's voice came through. I move in slowly, carefully, more silent than a shadow, and I'm grateful that Crystal moves just as quietly behind me. She has a talent for this kind of thing.

Finally, the room comes into view, and my heart jumps to my throat as I see Dakota there, and I lower my weapon immediately. She's sitting on the bed of a master bedroom, wringing her little hands and staring at the doorway with wide eyes. Her face gets excited and hopeful as soon as she sees me, and she gasps. I put a finger to my lips, then point to both sides of the door and raise my eyebrow. I pray she can figure out what I'm asking her.

"He's gone!" Dakota shouts, and a moment later, to prove her point, she sticks out her index finger toward the broken window behind her. I hesitate for half a second, not ignoring the possibility that Jake has got her convinced this is some kind of game, using my own daughter as bait in a trap to kill me at the last second.

But I have to trust Kota, and we don't have much time left.

I sweep into the room and round the corner, ready to see Jake standing there with a gun of his own.

The room's empty, except for me and Kota.

"Sweetie!" Crystal gushes as soon as she sees my shoulders relax, and she dashes into the room after me and receives Kota, who has her arms outstretched for her mom before she even starts moving.

"Mommy!" she cries as the two hug, and my heart swells to the point of hurting in my chest as I look at the two of them. I check the ensuite bathroom while they have a moment, but after making sure it's clear,

I can't help but approach them and hug them both in my arms.

I never thought of myself as having a paternal instinct. It just never crossed my mind, and I had no idea I'd be called on to make it come into action anytime soon. But here, standing with my girls in my arms...it couldn't feel more *right*. I even feel a tear threatening to spill from my eye.

"Did he hurt you, sweetie?" Crystal asks through sobs.

"No," Kota says simply. "I'm okay, Mommy."

Finally, I break the hug and kneel down at the bed to look at Dakota, who peers down at me from her mom's embrace.

"Kota, honey," I say in a soothing tone. "Where is Jake?"

Dakota looks over to the window and points to it again. I move around the bed, boots crunching on broken glass as I approach the window. What I see makes my heart jump to my throat.

There's a boat docked out there that, judging by the marks in the grass, got partially blown onto shore, and the dock is nothing but ruined driftwood all around, but it looks like someone has finally gotten the boat back into the water.

That someone is Jake, and he looks up at me with wide eyes as he starts to climb into the speedboat. As soon as we make eye contact, I see red.

I vault over the window and land in the wet grass

outside on both feet, and without a second thought, I start sprinting. Jake hops into the boat and begins starting the engine. I can hear him cursing the boat as I get closer by the second. Every drop of adrenaline rushing through my body is urging me forward, all united for one purpose: get the bastard who put my daughter in danger.

The boat engine starts up when I'm close enough to see the whites of Jake's eyes, and it starts to move away from the shore just a few second before I reach it. But no, I did not make it all the way down here just for Jake to get away from me by boat at the last second.

I jump.

With my running start, my body soars further than I feel like I've ever jumped. Just when I think with a sense of dread that I'm going to miss the boat, I catch the very edge of it, my legs sinking into the water while my arms hold me up.

Jake is no soldier, but even he knows how to think fast. And the second I'm half-on the boat, he acts on pure instinct, and he kicks the gun out of my hand. It flies up into the air and hits the water behind me, sinking into the depths as the boat takes off into the choppy waves.

Up above us, the sky is gray and bleak, but I can see storms all around us in a circle.

It's the eye of the storm, the one reprieve in the chaos. It's the one shot I've got at this.

Jake readies another kick, this time to my face, but my body springs into gear. I haul myself up out of the water and vault onto the boat, landing with a heavy, wet thud. Jake lunges at me, but I catch him and throw him backward, onto the boat as I crouch down to avoid getting tossed by the waves as the speedboat races out into the Roanoke Sound.

"You were just going to leave her?" I bark at Jake as we square off at each other. There's a look of fear mixed with anger in his eyes, while mine are nothing but pure rage. "She's a child, Jake! You left her to die!"

"You don't understand!" he shouts, fists shaking.

"No fucking explanation could be good enough for what you've done," I growl taking a step toward him. "You hurt my girl and you took Kota—*my child!*"

"Oh, so the absentee father finally figured it out?" he snarls.

"She told me!" I shout back. "Because it was *her* choice when to involve me in that part of her life, you selfish bastard!"

"Oh, *I'm* the selfish one?" he blurts incredulously. "I'm not the one who fucked off to the other side of the world to chase some dream! I'm the one who stayed here, taking care of that ungrateful bitch when she need-"

I cut him off with a solid punch to the jaw. He pulls back just in time to avoid taking the full brunt of it, but he still staggers long enough for me to tackle him.

That's when I see the knife he pulls out of his pocket.

We grapple as the boat speeds blindly out into the waters. A few times, it catches the choppy waves so hard that I worry the boat is about to tip over, but it holds out. I wrench Jake's arm around as he holds the knife out to try to get a stab at me, but the turbulent waters make it hard to take him on properly.

I feel a sting as his elbow catches me in the face, but I bring my forehead down on his nose and hear a crack that makes him scream. Blood starts running down his face, and he thrashes back and forth while I try to get the knife away from him. He brings it down in a stabbing arc, and I just narrowly avoid it — it stabs into the anchor rope of the boat, cutting a segment of it clean off.

Finally, the chaotic grappling gets out of hand, and I have to let him break away from me to avoid getting stabbed in the side. We both stand up in an instant. For a fraction of a second, I swear I could see us as teenagers again, play-wrestling innocently instead of at each other's throats.

"What the fuck happened to you?" I growl. "How long ago did the boy I know die and the man turn into this kind of evil?"

"I'm not the evil one," he spits back at me. "I'm the only one who cares!"

As he says that, tapping his chest with his free hand, we go over another choppy wave that bumps the boat hard. Jake curses, and my eyes go wide as I watch him stumble back...and over the side of the boat. I see something moving on the boat and realize his leg has gotten wrapped around part of the anchor cord in the struggle. Before I can stop it, the anchor of the boat follows Jake into the water, and I watch the cord slither out, cut from the boat by Jake's own knife.

I've barely had time to process what has happened when I rush to the boat's controls and slow it to a stop, turning around and looking at the wake behind me.

I've lost track of the exact spot where Jake went under the waves, and now, there's nothing left. No sign of either the friend I had or the villain he became.

Jake's gone.

I become aware of how hard I'm breathing, and I let my shoulders relax as I run my hand over my face and lean on the side of the boat. The water around me is still choppy and rough, but with the boat stopped, it feels like all the events of the day have come to just as much of a sudden halt. My brain can hardly keep up. I cast one last look at the general area where I last saw Jake, and when it really hits home that he's gone, I turn my back on it and go back to the boat's controls.

As I'm turning the boat around and looking back toward the house where my girls are, I see the two of them stepping outside and waving desperately. I feel a pang of worry, but then I realize they aren't waving at me. They're waving at the other sound I've been hearing from that direction.

A Coast Guard helicopter has made it out to the house, and it's circling, looking for a safe spot to land in the front yard of the house while we have a break in the eye of the storm. I feel relief wash over me, and I can't help but feel a smile on my face.

It's over.

We're safe.

And more importantly, my girls are safe.

"Mommy, look! It's landing!" Dakota shouts, wriggling in my arms and pointing up at the Coast Guard helicopter as it lowers to the soggy ground in the front yard of the Nag's Head home. The chopper sends a whirlwind spinning around it, kicking up dirt and debris. I turn and shield myself and Kota with my free arm.

I glance out toward the water, seeing Duncan still standing in the boat. Jake is nowhere in sight. I watched him topple out of the boat, and I can only imagine he's long drowned by now. It's a strange feeling, knowing that a man I was good friends with once upon a time is dead. I don't know how I am supposed to feel about this.

On the one hand, it saddens me to think of the Jake I used to know, but on the other hand, he's the same villain who tried to assault me, who kidnapped my precious daughter. Who tried to kill Duncan, the love of my life and father of my child.

I can't say I'm happy he's dead, of course, but I am relieved to have him out of the world. At least, my little world is better off without him.

The helicopter lands and two uniformed Coast Guards come jumping out. First, they rush over to Kota and me to drape a big blanket over my shoulders. There's a man and a woman, the latter of whom has a motherly, concerned look on her face. She leans in close to ask me a question, putting a hand on my shoulder, while the man keeps moving toward the lake.

"Are you alright, ma'am? Any injuries that you know of?" she questions.

I shake my head. "No. I don't think so. We're okay. It's Duncan I'm worried about. He's my— my boyfriend?" I say, almost asking myself. The woman smiles and nods.

"You mean the man in the boat out there? Don't worry. My team are bringing him in. You're all going to be okay. We'll get y'all out of here in no time," she assures me. "Come on, let's get you two into the chopper."

I look back over my shoulder toward the lake, relieved to see that she's right. There are two male members of the Coast Guard rushing to help Duncan. Satisfied with this, I dutifully get into the helicopter with Kota.

"Molly and Davey Neptune are in a bad way, too. Have you heard from them, yet?"

The woman nods to me, "Yes, we have people headed out that way now. We need to take advantage of the break in the storm," she says confidently before giving Dakota a warm smile.

"How are you feeling, sweetie? Thirsty? Hungry? Cold?" she asks in a gentle voice.

Dakota shrugs, still clearly in some degree of shock from the events of the day and night. "Little thirsty," she murmurs. "And I wet."

"Oh no," coos the woman. "Don't you worry, honey. I'll get you warmed up."

She hands me another blanket. I scoop up Kota and wrap her up in the blanket like a burrito, then sit her on my lap. She leans into me hard, almost clinging to me. I am so overjoyed to have her back with me again. When she was gone, it felt like a huge part of my heart was missing. I stroke her hair, feeling the curls start to dry out in the warm air of the helicopter cabin.

"My name's Marsha, by the way," the Coast Guard woman says, smiling. "Would you two like something warm to drink? I've got cocoa here."

"What do you think, sweetheart?" I ask Kota, leaning down. She nods vigorously.

"Yes, please!" she chirps, a dimpled grin on her sweet face.

Marsha gives us each a small styrofoam cup of

hot cocoa, which we sip while the other Coast Guards bring Duncan over to the helicopter. He climbs in beside me while they get into the cockpit, and my heart surges with joy to be reunited with him. As soon as the door is shut, Duncan scoots up to me and puts an arm around my shoulders, holding me tight.

"Oh, you're safe. Thank god," I murmur, resting my forehead against his shoulder.

He kisses the top of my head softly. "Of course, I am. These guys reeled me back in to safety. Besides, I've dealt with much worse situations than that," he says with a chuckle.

"I'll bet you have," Marsha says with a raised eyebrow as she takes out a first aid kit and pulls it onto her lap. "You're well-known in the military world. When we got the call that there was a situation out here, we had no idea we would find a celebrity."

"A celebrity?" I repeat incredulously.

Duncan shrugs. "I just do my job," he says simply.

One of the male Coast Guard members turns around in his seat ahead of us with a broad grin on his face. He can't be older than eighteen or nineteen with a baby face like that. He looks at Duncan almost adoringly. "No, sir. You're a legend. We used to talk about your missions in the barracks," he says, almost blushing.

"See?" Marsha says, laughing. "The boys and I are a little starstruck."

Duncan smiles graciously. "Well, I'm flattered, but today you all are the heroes for getting us out of there," he tells them. The young man in the front seat looks like he might just faint from such high praise. It's kind of adorable.

"I had no idea you were so famous," I whisper in Duncan's ear. He grins and shrugs it off again, like it's nothing. It hits me how excited I am to have him in my life with no barriers, no obstacles left between us. Jake is gone, Duncan knows all about Dakota, and now I'm learning more about what heroic life he's been leading in the four years we were apart.

Now there are only a few loose ends I need to tie up between us.

While Marsha is using the first aid kit to inspect Dakota for injuries— she does have a few cuts and light bruises, nothing serious— I decide that I'm done waiting for the right opportunity. I know what needs to be done, and I don't want to waste any more time. Four years is certainly long enough. So I take Duncan by the hand and lean in close to tell him my truth.

"I'm sure you know this already, but I'm going to say it anyway," I begin, my voice barely above a whisper. "I love you, Duncan. I never stopped loving you. And I never will. I'm sorry I let four years go by without telling you that. I should have known back then that you were the one. I was stupid. I was self-ish. I'm sorry."

He kisses me on the cheek. "Don't apologize, Crystal. You were only doing what you thought was best for me and for Dakota. You're an amazing mother. You are the woman of my dreams, and you always have been. I love you, too. More than anything in this world— well, except for maybe our daughter. As for those four years in between, I intend to make up for them by loving you extra hard for the rest of our lives. I promise you that. It'll be like no time at all has passed," he murmurs back, his low voice sending a delightful vibration down my spine.

With that settled, there's only one more thing to do. I look at Duncan and then at Dakota. He follows my drift and nods, his smile only getting broader. He squeezes my hand, helping to calm my nerves as my heart starts pounding. It's time to tell Dakota the truth. I don't want to waste another second of her life not knowing.

"Dakota, sweetheart," I begin softly. She looks up at Duncan and me, green eyes wide and innocent. Marsha seems to catch on that this is a big moment. She stops inspecting Kota, whose small cuts have already been cleaned up and bandaged.

"Go to your mommy, you're all done," Marsha tells her sweetly.

I reach out and grab my daughter, hoisting her

up into my lap to face us— her parents. Marsha turns away, presumably to give us some privacy. She's just old and wise enough to sense that we need a moment, and I'm grateful for that. Meanwhile, Kota stares up at me, waiting.

"What is it, Mommy?" she asks expectantly.

Duncan and I exchange looks of anticipation. "I have something important to tell you," I start off, stroking her soft face. "Something big. You ready?"

Kota grins, looking positively excited for the surprise.

"Duncan here… well, he's more than just an amazing man. He's more than just a hero," I tell her. "Kota, this is your daddy."

I watch the look on her face go from anticipation to shock to confusion and then, finally, to pure delight. She lets out a joyous giggle and reaches out to touch Duncan's jaw covered in five o'clock shadow, almost as though she has to touch him to believe he's real. Duncan leans forward to make it easier for her to reach, and he does the same to her, resting his massive palm against her soft cheek.

"Daddy," she mumbles, their identical green eyes locking in an intense stare. I feel tears burning in my own eyes to see them this way. The love is already there, I can feel it.

"My beautiful daughter," Duncan says softly. "I cannot wait to get to know you."

"You going to stay with Mommy and me?" she asks almost reverently.

Duncan smiles and nods slowly. "Yes. Of course, I am."

"Yay!" Kota exclaims, bounding over to plop down in her father's lap as though she's been doing it for years. Like no time has passed at all. Like he's been here all along.

Duncan hugs her close, grinning at me over her head. It's the most beautiful sight I have ever laid eyes on, and I can't believe my luck. Our family is whole again.

Six months later, driving up the clay driveway to our house never felt so good.

The drive up to our cozy little two-story place is so idyllic that I still can't believe it's all real. The road is bumpy and rocky, but I have the windows down, because on either side of me, the sights, sounds, and smells of nature are overwhelmingly beautiful. Crystal and I still love our hometown, but after everything that happened, we decided it was time to get away from the coast for a while.

That's what brought us to this quaint little slice of paradise outside Asheville, in the western part of the state.

I bring my car to a stop and climb out, breathing in the fresh, clean air. I've been all over the world, and I can say with confidence that the air around here is some of the freshest and cleanest that God's green earth has to offer. I look up at the tall trees that surround our house without fear that a hurricane is going to sweep through and start knocking them down.

On the contrary, I can take my time to appreciate the sounds of the various birds that make their home around here: titmouses, finches, cardinals, even crows are starting to sound like home, even though we've only been here a short time, in the grand scheme of things.

The last frost of winter was a few weeks ago, and while the air is still crisp and chilly, the sun is beating down on us, and it's bringing out everything good about springtime in North Carolina.

And that's a lot of good.

Crystal has adapted to life up here very well in a very short time. As I step out of my car to look at the circular clearing that serves as a yard, I see rows upon rows of the garden that she got started in such a short amount of time. The very first thing she did when we decided to move to the western part of the state was to research what all goes into gardening, planning one out, and getting all the equipment for it. I swear, she had her hands in the dirt before we even finished unpacking the boxes.

I make my way over to the soft soil, divided from the rest of the yard space by cute little wooden fencing no taller than my ankles. There are little dots of green all over the place— the seeds have just sprouted, since she planted everything right after the last frost. I put my hands on my hips and chuckle proudly at everything she's done. All the plants are labeled, meaning I know exactly what to look forward to from the fruits of her work: cucumbers, spinach, kale, turnips, and carrots are getting started in this particular patch of the garden. Closer to the house, she has a full spice rack's worth of herbs starting, and on the opposite side of the property from where I'm standing, she has a handful of fruiting vegetables starting.

In this part of the country, all you have to do to get something to grow is drop a seed somewhere. The soil is so rich and fertile that it'll give you everything you want and even more, and Crystal has proven to have a green thumb...so far. She insists that I dial back on showering her with praise until we actually have a salad or two on the dinner table.

That isn't the only perk to living up here. Going mushroom hunting in the trails winding around our house is the easiest thing in the world, and it gives us a great way to get Dakota out of the house. She'll be a wild child, we can tell, and I'm more than happy to encourage that by letting her explore this wild, beautiful neck of the woods as much as she wants.

I'm entranced by the beauty of Crystal's work when I hear the screen door open, and I turn to see her stepping out onto the porch with a warm smile on her face. She's wearing a very comfy outfit— one of my oversized t-shirts and a pair of black sweat-pants, neither of which hide the beautiful bump on her stomach.

She's pregnant again, and I couldn't be prouder.

"Now that's a sight that'll never stop being beautiful," I say to her as I approach the porch and wrap my hands around her hips, bringing her smiling face in for a kiss. She smells like the spices she cooks with, the smells that are soon going to get into the wood of the house and stick with us forever. I couldn't ask for a better home-smell.

"I was about to say the same thing," she says as we break the kiss. She lets her hands wander down from my broad, muscular shoulders to my biceps, and the smile on her lips is just as delectable as the one I saw on her face the night before I left for the Navy.

"How's our youngest daughter?" I ask, rubbing her stomach.

"Busy, today," she laughs, putting her hand over mine and squeezing it. I can't help but kiss her again, first on the lips, then over to her right cheek and down the side of her neck until she feels the tickle of my stubbly face and squirms away, giggling.

"The garden looks amazing."

"It hasn't even really started yet," she brushes the compliment off as usual, striding over to the edge of the porch to peer out at everything with a critical eye. "We'll be living off mushrooms for a while until

I actually see some results, but the motion camera you set up outside the property keeps getting triggered by deer, so don't be surprised if some uninvited guests help themselves. I might need to look into getting some chicken wire to keep it all safe."

"Consider it done," I say, jabbing a thumb back at our truck. "I've got to head out again later today to pick up some more chicken feed, since the first place I tried was out. I just wanted to stop in for lunch first. And because going a full three hours without seeing you is completely unacceptable," I add with a grin, and she blushes.

Despite getting everything settled here, I'm still a SEAL, which means I haven't just been sticking around this entire time. A lot has happened in six months.

Immediately after shit hit the fan in Kitty Hawk and we got to safety, I had to report back to my superiors. It would be an understatement to say they were surprised to hear about everything that went down in that storm. The Coast Guard seaman had been right when he said this one was big— it made national news, and on TV, Crystal and I were able to see just how lucky we'd been. We got hit by some of the worst the storm had to throw at us, and a lot of people weren't nearly so lucky. The damage was in the millions, and the relief effort was monumental.

My commanding officers gave me leave to aid with the relief effort, semi-officially. I stayed around for a month, digging out everything in my home-town that survived. It was a great, albeit awkward, way to reconnect with all the locals I knew and grew up with alongside Crystal. I made a lot of fast friends, though, and all the while, Crystal was at my side, volunteering.

I was absolved of anything I had to do to keep us alive. The testimony from Molly and Davey Neptune helped with that tremendously— they both pulled through, and last I heard, they were moving to Santa Fe to enjoy the rest of their retirement as far away from the possibility of hurricanes as humanly possible.

And I hear New Mexico is nice this time of year, so I've been thinking about planning a road trip out west with Crystal after we get settled here. That's a surprise, though.

Jake's death was ruled a boating accident, and our fight was considered self-defence on my part. It's impossible for me not to have mixed feelings about everything. Crystal does too. Both of us grew up knowing Jake as a close friend, and we always thought that's all he ever would be.

If he could just let friendship be a friendship and not see women as objects he can take if he puts enough time into them, he might still be alive today. But he chose a different path. Neither of us know when he started going down that road to ruin, but he chose it.

Crystal and I have had the conversation several times, late at night when we stare up at the starry sky and get thoughtful. Can we even say we miss the man he was before he started twisting his idea of Crystal in his head? Can we know where he went wrong? Does saying we miss that part of him come too close to absolving him of the twisted mentality he kept hidden for so long?

Those aren't fun questions to deal with, and we're still dealing with them. But what we do know is that we're safe now, and we will be from here on out.

"Daddy!"

I turn to see Kota racing around from the back yard, where the porch I built houses a bunch of potted plants that Kota has taken a liking to tending. For a child, she has amazing patience. That, or she just really likes playing with the bugs that get drawn to the plants. Either way, her hands haven't been clean for a solid hour ever since we moved here.

I scoop her up into my arms as soon as she bolts up the steps of the porch, and I swing her around as she giggles before I hug her tight and set her back down.

"Hey sweetie, find anything good today?"

"I found eight morels!" she says proudly. Mushroom hunting has become another fun hobby of hers.

"And one fun little blue mushroom that leaks this

weird, violet stuff that is really good at staining clothes," Crystal says with a half-annoyed laugh, tugging at Dakota's violet-stained dress. Kota just beams proudly, nodding affirmatively.

"Think we'll have to use the guide book to identify that one, it sounds new," I say, rubbing the back of my neck.

I'm still not used to her calling me Dad, but I've got to say, it's a good feeling. Ever since I saw the two of them, I've felt bonded to them, and that bond has only grown stronger with each passing day. Now, it's like I've been in Kota's life from the very start, and she loves me with every ounce of her little heart.

And I love her so much that it hurts.

"Why don't you go get the field guide, and we'll all look at it together, okay?" Crystal asks Kota, who nods excitedly and races inside. We smile at each other once she's gone, and then, Crystal's face falls just a bit.

"So," she goes on, "have you heard back from your people?"

"Yeah," I say, "I'm shipping out again next week. But it'll only be for two weeks, then I'm back again for a few more months."

She smiles at that, beautiful face glowing.

"Good," she says, wrapping her arms around my abs, "I'll make sure to have something special for you when you get back."

I grin and kiss her, and I want so badly to tell her all the things I have in store for her over the next year. My assignments are going to get more sporadic in the near future.

The huge engagement ring on Crystal's finger is a sign that I've got some big plans for us.

This is my family. This is the most important assignment, both in my heart and my soul. And I couldn't walk away for it for anything, even if I wanted to.

I protect my girls.

And with them at my side, every day is a new, wonderful adventure.

~

Thank you so much for reading! I hope you enjoyed <3 If you have a moment, please leave a review. Other readers are dying to know what you thought.

I have plenty more bad boy romance for you, so make sure you check out my other books on the next couple of pages, and sign up for my newsletter to be notified when I have a new release on the way!

~Alexis Abbott

ALSO BY ALEXIS ABBOTT

Romantic Suspense:

HITMEN SERIES:

Owned by the Hitman

Sold to the Hitman

Saved by the Hitman

Captive of the Hitman

Stolen from the Hitman

Hostage of the Hitman

Taken by the Hitman

The Hitman's Masquerade (Short Story)

THE KILLER TRILOGY:

Book 1: Killer for Hire

Book 2: Killer Desire

Book 3: Killer on Fire

SEXY SEALs

Sweetheart for the SEAL

Sights on the SEAL

HOSTAGES:

Stealing Her

The Assassin's Heart

Killing For Her

Abducted

Stepbrothers:

Ruthless

Criminal

Standalones:

Betting on Love

Hunter's Baby

I Hired A Hitman

Vegas Boss

Rock Hard Bodyguard

Innocence For Sale: Jane

Redeeming Viktor

Romance:

Falling for her Boss (Novella)

Most Wanted: Lilly (Novella)

Bound as the World Burns (SFF)

Erotic Thriller:

The Dangerous Men Series:

The Narrow Path

Strayed from the Path

Path to Ruin

ABOUT THE AUTHOR

Alexis Abbott is a Wall Street Journal & USA Today bestselling author who writes about bad boys protecting their girls! Pick up her books today if you can't resist a bad boy who is a good man, and find yourself transported with super steamy sex, gritty suspense, and lots of romance.

She lives in beautiful St. John's, NL, Canada with her amazing husband.

facebook.com/abbottauthor

twitter.com/abbottauthor

instagram.com/alexisabbottauthor

bookbub.com/authors/alexis-abbott

pinterest.com/badboyromance

youtube.com/AlexisAbbott

CONNECT WITH ALEXIS

Get an EXCLUSIVE book, **FREE** just as a thank you
for signing up for my newsletter! Plus you'll never
miss a new release, cover reveal, or promotion!

http://alexisabbott.com/newsletter

facebook.com/abbottauthor

twitter.com/abbottauthor

instagram.com/alexisabbottauthor

bookbub.com/authors/alexis-abbott

pinterest.com/badboyromance

ACKNOWLEDGMENTS

Thank you to my amazing Patrons. I'm constantly humbled and grateful for your support.

Ramona Cabrera
Melissa Hedrick
Virginia Swanson
Dawn Daughenbaugh
Don Doss
Stacie Currie

If you'd like to join them — and get my ebooks or paperbacks — you can find me here on Patreon.
https://www.patreon.com/alexisabbott

www.ingramcontent.com/pod-product-compliance
Lightning Source LLC
Chambersburg PA
CBHW021133190726
48288CB00008B/2628